7th

mis**fits** **inc.**

no. 6

hit and run

misfits inc.
no. 6

hit and run

mark delaney

PEACHTREE
ATLANTA

For my dear sister Theresa,
because she asked.
With lots of love…

A FREESTONE PUBLICATION

Published by
PEACHTREE PUBLISHERS LTD.
1700 Chattahoochee Avenue
Atlanta, GA 30318-2112

www.peachtree-online.com

Text © 2002 by Mark Delaney

Book and cover design by Loraine M. Joyner
Book composition by Melanie M. McMahon

Manufactured in the United States of America
10 9 8 7 6 5 4 3 2 1
First Edition

Library of Congress Cataloging-in-Publication Data
Delaney, Mark.
Hit and run / Mark Delaney.
   p. cm. -- (Misfits, Inc. ; no. 6)
Summary: When his mother, whom he has not seen in years, is falsely accused of a hit-and-run, Mattie finds himself and his fellow Misfits investigating a gang-controlled car-theft ring.

ISBN 1-56145-275-0
[1. Mystery and detective stories.] I. Title.
PZ7.D373185 Hi 2002
[Fic]--dc21   2002004832

E-mail the author at: misfitsink@aol.com

table of contents

Acknowledgments

Special Thanks to:

Detective Alex Bancroft of the Orange County Auto Theft Task Force,
my friend and brother-in-law, who checks me on police procedure
and makes sure Decker doesn't get a search warrant
unless he deserves one!

Amy Sproull Brittain and Vicky Holifield,
my loving and ferocious editors,
and all the editorial, production, and marketing staff at Peachtree,
whose skills, guidance, and creativity
have helped make the Misfits who and what they are.

Martin Reid
and his website www.martinreid.com
For his expert advice and information on
Larus Californicus, *the California Seagull*

prologue

getting the wheels right was the hardest part. Micah Washington held the model Corvette at the tips of his fingers. He rotated it under the desk lamp, squinting because the hundred-watt bulb was too bright and threw down irritating shadows. He frowned over the assembly directions and felt his tongue start to poke out from between his lips—a little kid's gesture he often made when he was trying to concentrate.

The wheels. Worry about the wheels. When he first started building model kits, Micah would squeeze out a big dollop of Testor's Model Cement onto the tips of the axles. But when he popped the wheels on, he found he'd glued the axles right in place. Micah's first three model cars all had wheels that wouldn't turn and hard, transparent glue balls at most of the joints.

He heard movement on the linoleum floor and looked up to see his five-year-old sister Tanaya shuffling toward him. "Whatcha doing?" she asked.

Micah squeezed a drop of Testor's onto a sheet of newspaper. Then he dipped the point of a toothpick into the drop and rubbed just a tiny bit of the glue onto the tip of one axle. "Building a 1961 Corvette convertible," he said without looking up. "With scoops on the sides."

"What's are scoops?"

Micah pointed to a splash of white that started from behind the car's front wheel and arced across a portion of the door. "This," he said.

"What's it do?" Tanaya asked.

Micah paused. He brought the model closer and studied the scoop for several moments. Then he looked at his sister again. "Go away," he said.

Instead of leaving, Tanaya drew nearer, her small hand reaching into the box of model parts. She pulled out the windshield and propped it in her eye, like an old man wearing a monocle. "Can I put a window in?" she asked.

"Nope."

She pouted. "How come?"

"Because," Micah said, "you'll get glue on your fingers and smudge it all over the window and ruin it. Then you'll lick the glue off and die."

Tanaya's eyes widened. "Moooooommmm!"

Micah's mother, Corie, stood a few feet away in the kitchen, spooning macaroni and cheese into plastic bowls. It wasn't a kitchen really. The apartment manager called it a *kitchenette*. And the green card table where he sat building his model was a *dinette*. The apartment consisted of one room. His mom could hear every word he and his sister were speaking.

"Micah," she said, "do not tell your sister she's going to eat glue and die. Now take your Mustang off the table, so we can eat."

"Corvette," Micah muttered to himself. He scooped the unused model pieces back inside their cardboard box and laid the unfinished model on top of them. He then slipped the lid back on the box and paused for a moment to examine the painting on the cover. A red Corvette tore down a city street, light glinting off its windshield and front bumper. The background of the picture was a haze of streaky speed lines.

"Micah!" snapped his mother, and he slid the box under his chair.

He ate dinner in silence. Tanaya chattered about something she had colored that afternoon and scurried from the table to find it. Mom asked Micah a couple of questions about school—*What did you learn in English today? Do you have any homework?* Micah grunted some answers.

He was eating a chocolate chip cookie for dessert when he heard the squeal of rubber burning tracks onto pavement. Micah rushed to the apartment's only window and stared down into the street. His mother ran to join him, and Tanaya crawled onto a chair so she could see too. A car barreling down Eighth Avenue fishtailed, ran up onto the sidewalk, and plowed into a pair of metal garbage cans. They flew into the air and landed behind the car in a loud clatter and spray of garbage. As he watched, Micah felt his mother's hand grip his shoulder.

4   Old Mr. Underwood, who let even the little kids call him Joseph, stood on the sidewalk below. Micah watched the old man step back as the car raced toward him—it must have been doing sixty. It jumped the curb again and slammed into Mr. Underwood. Micah watched as though it were a movie playing in slo-mo, his sister's shrieks an odd sound effect behind him. He felt his mother's arms wrap around his chest. She tried to draw him away, but at ten he was already nearly as strong as she was, and he'd planted his feet. Mr. Underwood rolled up the hood of the car, then over the roof and trunk, before falling again to the pavement. Micah saw the whole scene frame by frame, a series of still-clicks, and then it all speeded up again. A woman in another apartment screamed. The car sped away.

"Oh, my God," said Micah's mom. "Oh, my God."

Micah felt her arms leave him. He heard her footsteps cover the few feet into the kitchenette and the faint tones as she punched three buttons on the phone. A crowd gathered below, and minutes later an ambulance arrived.

A knock came at the door. When Micah's mom answered it, two uniformed policemen looked back at her from the hallway. One of them, a woman with brown hair pulled back in a tight bun, asked if they could come in. Had Corie seen the accident? The cop held out a clipboard and wanted Micah's mom to fill out a statement describing the whole thing. "Can you tell us about the car?" she asked.

Corie Washington shook her head. "It—it all happened so fast. A car—blue, I think—hit that man."

Micah walked toward his mother, eyeing the two policemen as he did. The woman was scribbling something down in a small spiral notebook. When she finished, she looked up at her partner, a tall, narrow-faced cop whose gleaming uniform cap made him look a little silly, Micah thought—like a kid playing policeman. "We're not going to get anywhere if no one got a good look at the car," muttered the woman.

"It was a Chevy Malibu," Micah said.

Both cops turned and stared at him. "What?" said the man.

"Chevy Malibu," said Micah. "1982 model. Blue. The license plate number was 1XGP394."

The woman grunted and half smiled. She wrote the description down in her notebook. "Are you positive?" she asked. "It's important that you're absolutely sure."

Micah nodded.

"What's your name?" she asked.

"Micah Washington."

She wrote that down too. "Okay, Micah," she said. "Thank you. That's great. Did you know the man who was hurt?" she asked.

Micah nodded again.

"Well," she said, "we're going to do our best to find the person who did this to Mr. Underwood. Does that make you feel better?"

Micah stared at her, blinking. "His name was Joseph," he said.

chapter
one

Wednesday, 7:59 A.M.
Bugle Point High School

mattie Ramiro's first period class began with the sound of footsteps just outside the door. A knuckle rapped on the window, and when Mrs. Molina opened the door, a hand fed a slip of paper to her through the narrow opening. The teacher glanced at the note, nodding to the faceless messenger. Her eyes then scanned the classroom, settling in a very long gaze…on Mattie Ramiro. She strode down the row where he sat and handed him the note. *Oh great*, Mattie thought. *Merry Christmas in March.*

Mattie had never received a note from the office, other than the time he had tried to fix a drinking fountain and ended up breaking the pipe underneath it, sending a spray of water down the long, linoleum-floored hallway of the D-wing. So now he felt warmth pouring into his face. He was fair-skinned, and so blushed a plum color. Thirty pairs of eyes stared at him.

He looked at the name at the top of the message—

Rebecca Kaidanov. *Rebecca! Maybe this isn't so bad after all,* he decided. And the words, too, seemed innocent.

> *Need to talk to you and the other Misfits.*
> *Will stop by school at 3:00. Meet you near*
> *the flagpole.*
> *—Rebecca K.*

The words were on a square message slip used by the school's front office: Astrobrite paper, so glaringly pink it almost hurt Mattie's eyes to read it. The words Important Message appeared in boldfaced type at the top, and below were spaces for the time and date of the call, the name of the caller, and the caller's number. Below that was a series of check boxes. The Urgent box had a check in it.

Mattie refolded the note and tapped it against his desktop. Rebecca Kaidanov was a reporter for the *Bugle Point Courier.* When Mattie and his friends had uncovered a plot to kill off a rare species of kingfisher, Rebecca had written a story about them—but certain people had wanted her to keep her mouth shut, so she got fairly roughed up in the process. Some time later, Mattie and his friends had learned the truth surrounding a missing protest singer and the bombing that had ended his career. With that story, Mattie recalled, Rebecca had earned her first front-page byline.

"Back to work everybody," said Mrs. Molina.

Mattie stuffed the message in his pocket and reached

for his spiral notebook. Mrs. Molina always began the English 10 class by having students write a short essay response to a question. She had, as usual, scrawled the topic across the dry-erase board. Mattie's stomach sank as he read it: *In the poem "The Road Not Taken," the speaker remarks on how the choices he made in the past have brought him to the life he leads today. Imagine your life as you would like it to be twenty years from now. What choices are you making now that might affect your future? What choices might you later regret?*

Twenty years from now? Mattie thought. *I have enough trouble keeping up with tomorrow's homework assignments.* Sighing, he reached for a pen. First off, he imagined a world in which there were no Robert Frost poems. However, knowing Mrs. Molina, he would have to move past that point pretty quickly. *Twenty years from now,* he scribbled, *I will single-handedly save the planet Earth from an alien invasion. I will receive the Nobel Prize for discovering a cure for acne. I will end world hunger by making the school open up an extra snack line in the cafeteria…*

A few moments later the classroom door creaked open, and a girl with short, spiky blond hair strode into the room. She said nothing, just signed the tardy sheet at Mrs. Molina's desk and slid into her seat. The girl—her name was Heather something—dropped her backpack to the floor with a tremendous *thunk,* then folded her arms in front of her and stared at the board sullenly.

After Mrs. Molina had collected the essays, she rubbed her hands together briskly. "Today, class," she boomed, "we will begin the Shakespeare projects I discussed earlier in the week." She handed the first person in each row a stack of sheets describing the assignment. Mattie took one and glanced at it as he passed the remainder of the stack to the classmate behind him.

The assignment was pretty much what he expected. Mrs. Molina grouped students in twos and asked each pair to paraphrase a scene from *The Tragedy of Julius Caesar*. She began—her loud voice occasionally rattling the door—to call out the pairs she had assigned. "Amy Attleberry and Philip Manetti...Jeremy Yuan and Stephen McKnight...Mattie Ramiro and Heather Connelly..."

Mattie didn't hear the rest. His face warmed, and a tingling started in his shoulders and traced its way to the tips of his fingers. Heather Connelly. That was the girl's name. *Greeaaat,* he thought. Here they were starting one of most heavily weighted assignments of the semester, and he just got paired with a student who missed class practically every other day. Mattie couldn't recall her ever speaking in class, except for a few times at the very beginning of the semester when she responded to the roll call too softly, and Mrs. Molina had to repeat her name. He looked across the room. The girl was slumped over with her face buried in her hands. She lifted her head and, without so much as a glance at Mattie, scooped up her books and shot past him, then ran out the classroom door.

Mrs. Molina strode to the door and yanked it open. When she closed it behind her, she closed it quietly. Mrs.

10 Molina had a fondness for loud noises. When she closed the door gently, you knew she was angry.

Mattie felt each second tick by. *Mrs. Molina pairs Heather with me…and then the girl walks out of the classroom?* He tapped his knuckles against the top of his desk. He took out his pen—four buttons, one for each color—and disassembled it, leaving the pieces scattered on his desktop. Finally, having run out of distractions, he threw up his hands and grinned at the class. "That's right, folks," he said. His voice tore right through the uncomfortable silence. "She didn't wanna work with me, so she walked right out. Bet we'll all be talking about that for the rest of the semester, don'tcha think?" He held an imaginary microphone, faking an announcer's voice. "What are you gonna do now, Mattie?" Then, in his own voice: "I'm going to Disneyland!" He cupped his hands and hissed into them. It sounded like a vast audience applauding.

"Perfect pair," someone whispered. "Gone and goner." Several kids laughed.

Moments later the teacher opened the door again and guided Heather back into the room. The girl, her eyes red, took the desk next to Mattie. Mrs. Molina lowered her gaze and let it pan, radarlike, across the classroom. "Get to work, everybody," she said.

Heather scooted her desk closer. "Sorry," she said. "It wasn't about you. I'm—I'm just not having a good day." She sniffled and ran a finger underneath her nose. Then she averted her eyes from Mattie and reached for her copy of the handout. "So what's this about?"

Mattie had had one class with her in middle school. She had been cute, bright, always answering questions. Yet now, sophomore year in high school, Heather's hair and clothing were one step above a total mess. Her face was full and round. She wore baggy jeans, the ends torn and frayed because they were too long and she'd been walking on them. Her sweatshirt was huge, wrinkled, and fell almost to her knees. A yellow stain marked the front of it. She was sickly pale. The freckles across her nose were more noticeable than he remembered. Her skin had broken out.

"What are you staring at?" she demanded, finally looking at him.

"Let's just get this done," muttered Mattie.

According to the handout, they had to find a scene in *Julius Caesar,* put it in their own words, and memorize it. Then they had to perform it in front of the class.

"How about the scene with Caesar and Calpurnia?" Mattie suggested. "You know, when she tells him about her nightmare?"

Heather wasn't even on the right page in the text. She flipped the pages so that they crackled, stopping when she reached the Shakespeare unit. She said nothing about Mattie's idea.

"…Or not," said Mattie.

While the rest of the class chattered excitedly, buzzing with ideas, Mattie struggled with his stony partner. He suggested two more scenes. She shrugged. He suggested *she* could pick the scene. He fidgeted, his foot tapping angrily in the silence. After a while, he could no longer

12 stand to just sit there. He reached for the pieces of his pen and reassembled them. Then, holding it between thumb and forefinger, he made the pen vanish. A moment later it reappeared. Smiling, he did the trick over and over, staring vaguely as the pen popped into his hands, popped out, and popped in again. Finally, it must have reappeared one too many times. Heather reached over and snatched it away.

"Enough," she said. "I've heard about you. Next thing it'll be card tricks, and I'm really not in the mood."

He considered that a moment. "Can I get my pen back?"

"Whatever," she said in a dull voice. *Either she's tired,* Mattie thought, *or just really unhappy.* She gave him the pen and sniffled. Mattie ran his suggestions by her again, and after a moment's conversation, they turned to the scene where Brutus talks to his wife, Portia. Miraculously, over the next twenty minutes, they managed to compose a short scene. It was one of those lame efforts calculated to earn a C, Mattie knew, but he figured that a B or an A required more energy and will than Heather possessed. Then Heather surprised him: "Portia's crazy," she said. "She jabs a knife into her leg to make a point to her husband. I like that."

Well, Mattie thought, *that's a contribution.*

With three minutes left in the period, Mattie could feel the noise level in the room ratcheting up. The room felt rowdy, freer as students finished their work and began aimlessly chatting. Mattie scooted his desk back into its row, zipped his text and his notebook into his backpack, and once again averted his eyes from Heather. He heard her backpack *thunk* against the desktop, heard the zipper buzz.

"I remember you from middle school," Mattie blurted. "You used to smile a lot." The words came out so quickly, Mattie was unable to stop them. His eyes met Heather's.

"What?" she asked. The single word was harsh and clipped. She didn't look at him, only stuffed her books into the bag.

Now that he had gotten the first words out, he couldn't stop himself. "You answered questions in class all the time. You did really well. I didn't see your grade on our last test, but I could see the red ink all over it even from here." He knew he was being rude, but he pressed on. "What happened?"

Heather paused. For the first time Mattie had the sense she was really looking at him. Her eyebrows furrowed, but she was smiling too, as though she were both amazed and charmed by the fact that Mattie had asked such a stupid question. "You mean you don't know?" she asked.

Mattie shook his head.

Heather stood and slung her backpack over her shoulder. "I had a kid is what happened," she said.

Then the bell rang and she was gone.

8:52 A.M.

Like lurching zombies in some cheesy horror movie, one very large boy appeared from behind a bank of lockers,

14 and another one came from a classroom that lay just ahead. The zombies were wearing Abercrombie & Fitch khakis and letterman jackets.

Football players.

When Peter Braddock saw them, he stopped. They were the biggest players on the team. Peter sensed instantly the makings of an ambush, an attempt to catch him by surprise—though Peter was never very surprised when others ganged up on him.

Students in the crowded hallway pushed past the group, slamming locker doors, laughing, chattering loudly with friends. Anything that happened in the next few moments would be lost amid the commotion. "Smart," Peter said. "The busiest hallway in school." People jostled to get through to their classes. Peter couldn't run away even if he wanted to.

As the football players drew closer, Peter struggled to remember their names but couldn't. He didn't hang out with athletes much, and with their hair shaved down to almost nothing—something all the varsity players did— he had a difficult time latching onto ways to distinguish them. "We just want to have a little conversation," one said, grinning.

Peter forced himself to remain calm. His father was a special agent for the FBI, and Peter had long ago learned—or perhaps he had been born with—his father's abilities to observe and deduce. His eyes scanned the football players: He saw greenish ink lines on one boy's wrist, poking out from the sleeve of a jacket. *A tattoo,* Peter concluded. *A dinosaur? No, a dragon.* He noted a tiny hole in the guy's left nostril, surrounded by reddened skin. The boy had removed his nose ring so he wouldn't violate the school dress-code policy. The other one shifted his weight nervously from one foot to the other. A white plastic object poked out of his pocket. *An inhaler,* mused Peter. *Either this one's asthmatic, or he has really bad allergies.* "You know," the one with the tattoo said, stepping closer, "nobody likes a guy who goes out of his way to get someone in trouble."

Peter held his hands up, palms out. "Hey," he said, "if you're here to warn me that you're going to beat the snot out of me later, fine—but at least get your facts straight. I did *not* tell on Jeremy Roulston."

"Did you know Roulston is an all-state player who happens to be averaging twelve catches, almost two hundred and forty yards, and two touchdowns every game?" the boy demanded.

"He was my chemistry lab partner," Peter replied. "And he was letting me do all the work while he sat back and did nothing."

The guy doing all the talking drew nose to nose with Peter. "So you whined to the teacher."

Peter stepped back to put a little space between him and the football player. He had an irrational urge to laugh in the guy's face but bit the inside of his cheek to stop himself. "Listen," he said. "I didn't say a word about Jeremy. All I did was ask if I could work on the lab by myself, and the teacher said yes."

"Which left Jeremy without a lab partner," said the guy.

"And let me guess," said Peter. "He never did the lab."

The football players closed in on Peter. A few students must have noted their threatening posture, because several stopped talking and glanced at the scene as they passed.

"He got a D on his progress report," said the other guy, finally deciding to join in. He took out his inhaler, popped off the cap, and sprayed a dose of medicine into his mouth. Peter could smell it when the boy spoke. "Which meant that his grades dropped below a C average."

"Right," said Peter. "And so he didn't meet the eligibility requirements."

League rules required athletes to maintain a C average and have no failing grades. The principal, Mr. Steadham, had expanded that policy so that it applied to school-wide activities as well—from band to theater arts. Everyone knew the rule. "So," Peter went on, "Roulston doesn't get to play until next grading period. That's *my* fault?"

The guy with the tattoo whipped off his jacket and let it drop to the floor, revealing the full dragon, which ran from his elbow to the strap of his wristwatch. Peter thought the whole tough guy display was pretty pathetic. At the same time, it sent a blast of adrenaline down Peter's spine and out to the tips of his fingers. Any guy stupid enough to think that throwing his jacket on the ground and showing off a tattoo made him look tough was also stupid enough to start throwing punches right in the hallway at school. Peter took another step back. A pair of hands hit his shoulder blades and shoved him forward again.

Then a figure appeared alongside Peter—in fact, it loomed over him. Of course, he knew who it was even before he turned and saw the clarinet case. The tingling Peter felt in his arms fizzled, like sparks from an electrical fire spitting one last time before dying out.

Jake Armstrong grinned. "Hey, Peter," he said. He nodded a careful greeting to each of the football players. "Will…." Then, before addressing the other football player, the one with the tattoo, Jake bent down and picked the jacket up off the floor. His tone went icy. "And Mike Gilbert. How's it going, Mike?" He tossed the jacket so that it slapped sharply into the boy's stomach. "I see you're on varsity again. Congratulations."

No one spoke. Jake was six foot two and a powerful two hundred pounds. Will threw a glance at the one named Mike Gilbert. Gilbert, apparently less certain now about the odds in this fight, tugged his jacket back on and shook his head. "You know," he said, "I get so sick of you *smacks*."

Peter stiffened. "Smack" was a word for any student for whom good grades and studying came easily. Last year someone had soaped it across the windshield of his prized '67 VW convertible.

Gilbert sneered at Peter. "You think you're so smart. Like you're so much better than the rest of us."

Peter tapped his finger against his chin, looking at each of the football players in turn. "A football field," he said, "is a hundred yards long, but how many yards wide is it?"

"Fifty," said Gilbert. "Everyone knows that."

"Fifty-three and one-third," corrected Peter. "One hundred and sixty feet. Our quarterback, Barry Concannon, can throw a football sixty yards, but he keeps underthrowing Roulston on that forty-yard post pattern your coach likes to call on third and long. Know why?"

Neither of the football players spoke. Last week, Peter knew, their coach had called this very play with seconds left in the game. Roulston had been wide open, only to have the pass bounce off the back of his right knee.

"It's because Barry is left-handed." Peter went on. "He runs to his left just before throwing, and Roulston's pattern takes him almost to the far side of the field. To gain forty yards, Barry has to throw the length of the *diagonal* from corner to corner, which is—" Peter did some quick calculations in his head. *The square of the hypotenuse is equal to the sum of the square...* "—sixty-six and two-thirds yards. Tell Concannon not to peel to his left, and tell Roulston to shorten the pattern a bit, and you'll win more games."

"You don't know football," spat Gilbert.

Peter shrugged. "This is geometry."

The two players huddled together. Will pulled a folded sheet of paper from his pocket and spread it out on the floor. "See?" he said. He started drawing *X*s and *O*s, followed by a long angled line to indicate Jeremy Roulston's failing post pattern. But Mike Gilbert remained unmoved. He stood to one side, glaring at Peter and fiddling with the zipper on his jacket.

"Come on," Peter said to Jake. "Let's go."

They headed down the hall toward Peter's locker. When Peter shifted his heavy backpack from one shoulder to the other, he couldn't help noticing that, while his backpack bulged with a nine-hundred-page literature text, a Warriner's grammar book, a Permabound copy of *The Scarlet Letter,* and three spiral notebooks, Jake carried only a six-pound clarinet case.

As they made their way through the crowded hallway, neither of them spoke. But Jake wore an odd half-smile and kept stealing glances at Peter, which Peter found inordinately annoying.

"Okay…" said Peter. He had known it was coming. It was just a matter of which of his friends decided to tease him first.

"So you *have* heard."

"Byte told me."

"Ah…" said Jake. He paused. "Well then, I'm surprised you're not talking about it, since she *was*…you know—"

"Change the subject," said Peter.

"Sure," said Jake. More silence, then: "I mean, I'm just surprised—"

"Is this a new subject?"

"No."

"Then I'm not talking."

Peter spun the dial on his locker.

"She likes you," said Jake.

"Oh, do you *think?*" Peter yanked on his locker handle. "Ow!"

Peter's thumbnail had caught on the sharp edge of the handle. He shook the hand, and then stuck his thumb in his mouth. Jake started to speak again, but Peter held up his free hand, silencing him.

It took a moment or two for Peter to dump his English books and exchange them for trig and Survey of American History. As he was sliding the trig book into his backpack, he heard a light humming noise come up from behind him. The hallway had thinned out as students made their way to class, but a few students remained, and Peter heard them laughing. He turned to find a ten-inch-long radio-controlled car racing toward him. It buzzed as it approached, curving to make its way around moving students, and stopped three inches in front of his shoes. A lever fell forward, and the car deposited two folded slips of paper at Peter's feet. Each slip bore an emblem—a circle intersecting a square. It had been Peter's design, the two shapes suggesting a round hole and square peg, two things that could never fit together. It had become the symbol for Misfits, Inc., the group he had formed with his friends. Peter picked up the notes, handing one to Jake. The car, its mission accomplished, executed a perfect Y-turn and sped off, no doubt with a note for the group's remaining member.

"It's from Mattie," said Peter.

Jake unfolded his note. "How in the world did you guess?" he asked.

"He wants us to meet him at the flagpole after school. Doesn't say why."

He folded the note back up and stuck it in his pocket. The two headed off to their next classes.

"Getting back to our first subject—" said Jake.

"I'm not listening," said Peter.

"She's gonna get you, you know."

Fifth period

Eugenia "Byte" Salzmann pursed her lips and made a sound like that of air flubbering out of the end of a balloon. Of all the thoughts that could be occupying her mind, trigonometry was at the bottom of the list. She glanced around the room. Other students seemed to have little trouble concentrating. Some stared down with their noses inches from their desktops, pencils scritching across graph paper. Others fussed over calculators with tiny graphing screens. Sighing, Byte could only stare helplessly at her laptop monitor, which glowed with her lame attempt at wrestling with trigonometric identities. She rarely used paper or a calculator. Byte did all her schoolwork on her laptop, and the device never left her side. The problem staring up at her involved calculating the values of various angles within a group of oddly intersecting triangles. Worse, the shape of the triangles changed depending on how she plotted them. Sometimes they were sharp and lean, almost spikes, and under other values they were broad pyra-mids. *Augh!*

Byte closed out her trig program and decided she'd finish the work that night.

Just to keep her mind empty Byte began doodling with her computer's draw function. She colored the bottom half of her screen forest green. A field of grass, she sup-posed. The top half of her screen she filled with blue. Probably a sky.

The reason she couldn't concentrate, she knew, was Jake Armstrong.

Byte tried to shut out the image of Jake that came to her mind, but she couldn't. For months Byte had been doing all she could to send the right messages—the smiles, the warm hellos, the supportive pats on the arm, the I'm-*soooo*-glad-you-called brightness on the tele-phone. She had even sat in Jake's garage while he worked on his car, downloading directions for replacing a head gasket. But she finally had to face facts. Jake was a lug, as dense as they came. Worse, he was as shy with girls as she was with guys.

Within the green field, Byte drew a vertical line that had a slight curve to it. She topped the line with a small circle, which she filled in with yellow. Then she absently drew another line that curled outward from the circle and swept back. This curved line formed an ellipse, which she then filled in with white. She drew another, similar ellipse, and another, until her drawing took on the appearance of something familiar. Byte smiled to herself. *It's a daisy.*

Even if Jake *were* interested in her, Byte thought—and so far he had given her no reason to think he was—he likely wouldn't say anything.

She clicked on one of the daisy's petals with her mouse and dragged it away so that it lay by itself in the green field.

Byte realized, too, that her problem with Jake might have a deeper complication. That complication was Peter Braddock. Just as Byte had been sending messages to Jake about her feelings, Peter had been sending some messages of his own. To her. Byte frowned at this thought. She dragged another petal away and left it near the other one.

She liked Peter. She really did. He was a friend. A *close* friend. She wouldn't dream of hurting him. What if…what if he told her straight out how he felt? Byte felt a slight twinge of panic, then dismissed the thought. She had to be wrong. She wasn't reading Peter correctly; that had to be it. And when he smiled at her goofily, or when his hand accidentally brushed hers then shot away— well, there just had to be another explanation. With that thought, Byte glanced once again at her computerized doodle. She banished three more of the petals.

She looked at the last remaining petal, finally bored with her game, and dragged it away too. The yellow center of the now-shorn daisy stared back at her—a jaundiced eye, watching.

Byte heard snickering behind her. She spun around and saw Aimee Louvier—a girl with black lipstick, black nail polish, heavy black eyeliner, and ghostly pale skin—

24 staring at her. Aimee's shaggy black hair tumbled to her waist.

"He loves you," said Aimee.

"Huh?" said Byte. Her cheeks tingled. She would have put on a mask of indignation—*What do you mean? I don't know what you're talking about!*—but apparently the cat was not going back into that particular bag. How had Aimee known?

The Goth-queen shrugged. She pointed at the digital daisy petals lying in the digital grass. "I don't know who it is, but he loves you. I counted, and Mother Nature never lies."

Byte spun back around and stared at her computer screen. She thought of slamming down the monitor, deleting the evidence, but she was too late to hide anything from Aimee Louvier. To the witch-girl, the daisy petals had spoken.

When the final bell of the day rang, Byte hauled herself from her seat, nearly staggering under the combined weight of her backpack and computer bag. She forced herself through the crowded hallway, wincing at the metallic slam of a locker door. Her head ached. Her wire-framed granny glasses were dirty and blurred her vision. When a passing student—who did not so much as utter an "excuse me"—bumped into her, the glasses slipped to the end of her nose. Byte muttered under her breath and crinkled her nose to set them straight.

That's when a radio-controlled car pulled up and

parked at her ankles. Its front end spat out a note bearing a Misfits, Inc. emblem. A little plastic driver raised his arm in a little plastic wave. A sound chip said "Hel-lo, Byte," in Mattie Ramiro's voice. Then the car, humming as it shifted into reverse, shot back in the direction from which it had come.

Byte snatched the note from her shoe top, jammed the trig book in her locker, and slammed shut the locker door.

She read the note and, five minutes later, found the others waiting for her in the parking lot. Peter, Jake, and Mattie stood next to a pinkish-purplish Geo Tracker. Standing beside the Tracker was a woman with coarse, dark hair and striking blue eyes. *Rebecca!* Byte waved at the group and began to walk faster, pressing her hand against her computer bag to keep it from slapping against her hip.

"Hello, Byte," said the reporter.

Byte grinned at the way the woman clicked off the hard *T* in her name. Rebecca had come to the United States as a child from her home in the old Soviet Union, and traces of her Russian accent lingered in her speech.

"What have I missed?" asked Byte.

"We've been *waiting* for you," said Peter. "Putting off the good part because you were late." He smiled broadly at Rebecca. "Now we can stop talking about the weather, right?"

"Hey," said Byte, "I'd have gotten here sooner if a certain little *bug*—" Here she glared at Mattie. "had sent a note to me earlier. What happened, Mattie?"

Mattie shrugged. "I was busy, okay? I promise same-day service. You want something better, call FedEx."

Byte smacked him on the shoulder. "Anyway. What brings you out here, Rebecca?" she asked.

"Business for Misfits, Inc.," Rebecca replied. The reporter smiled at all of them, but the smile flattened a bit, Byte thought, when it turned to Mattie. "Someone needs your help."

"Who?" asked Jake.

"Well, this is really awkward." Staring off in the distance—and clearly refusing to meet their eyes—Rebecca took a deep breath. "She made me promise not to tell."

Peter, Byte could see, was intrigued. He was smiling at the reporter, his eyes narrowing, searching for clues in her expression. "Is it someone we know?" he asked.

No answer.

"Rebecca," said Jake. "Come on, tell us *something*."

Peter was nodding, gathering his thoughts. "Whatever this is about," he announced, "my guess is that it affects one of us personally. A stranger might have asked to remain 'anonymous,' but Rebecca used the word 'promise.' A promise is intimate, it's personal." He took a moment, apparently assessing his logic and finding it satisfactory. "Okay, I'm in," he said. "If the others are."

"I'm in," said Mattie.

Jake and Byte nodded as well.

"Then let's go," said Rebecca. "This person needs help as soon as possible. I can take you right now."

Byte's hand flew to her computer bag. "Oh, but I'll have to go back inside and send an Instant Message to my mom," she said, "to let her know I'll be late."

"Yeah," said Peter, "and the rest of us Neanderthals will have to use the pay phone. We'll be back in a few minutes." As they headed toward the school building, Mattie nudged Peter's elbow. Byte could hear the two whisper. "Hey, it's Thursday," Mattie said. "Is your mom making pork chops for dinner?"

"I don't know, Mattie," said Peter.

"What do you mean?" Mattie cried, the whispering forgotten. "She always makes pork chops on Thursday. The ones with the spicy-crumbly stuff on them. It's tradition. She makes chops, I mooch."

They returned several minutes later. Rebecca opened the door to her Tracker and threw the seatback forward. "I think we can all fit, if we squeeze in," she said. Peter, Byte, and Mattie clambered into the back seat. Jake, because of his size, rode shotgun in the front.

"So where are we going?" Peter asked.

The car's engine roared to life. Byte heard the parking brake *cha-chunk* as the reporter released it.

"The county jail," Rebecca said.

chapter two

The walls at the county jail were a dull, institutional green. An armed police officer, overweight and clearly close to retirement, met them at the door and gestured them in. Rebecca whispered a few words to the man. He nodded and pointed toward another guard—a thick, muscular woman who sat behind a glass window. Her expression was flat, emotionless.

Everyone, Peter noted—Rebecca, the elderly guard, the woman behind the window—spoke in subdued tones, as though the building were a library or funeral home. The woman thrust forward a cheap clipboard, a ballpoint pen attached to it with string. Clipped to the board was a sign-in sheet. When all five had signed in, the guard examined it.

"Does this say Saltmann or Sartmann?" she asked. In reply, Peter handed the woman one of the Misfits' business cards. She held it under her desk lamp, squinting.

**misfits inc.
investigations**

Mysteries are no mystery to us!

Jake Armstrong   Matthew Ramiro
Peter Braddock   Byte Salzmann

"Oh, you're a *businessman*," said the woman, rolling her eyes. "Sorry to keep you waiting, Mr. Gates."

Here Rebecca stepped forward, lending the credibility of an adult presence. After a few whispered words, the guard pointed Rebecca down a long hallway. Peter looked at the others: *Any idea what's going on?* They were as lost as he was.

The Misfits followed Rebecca through a doorway. The eerie quiet persisted. Peter heard no raised voices except for one—a distant, crying moan coming from a prisoner in one of the cells. Peter thought it sounded like wind over a lake at night.

The hallway was lit by bare fluorescent bulbs that hung from the ceiling. Occasionally one of the bulbs flickered and buzzed as electricity arced through its connections. The Misfits followed Rebecca to a door that opened into a small room. Peter recognized it as a consultation room, a place where prisoners could meet with their attorneys and hold private, privileged conversations. Peter had heard that nothing spoken here could be used against a prisoner at a later trial.

"Hey, is this one of those rooms the prisoners always use to talk to lawyers on TV?" whispered Byte.

"I think so," Peter murmured.

Mattie's voice rang out, echoing in the windowless room. "Are we, like, not supposed to talk or something?" he asked. Peter, struggling not to laugh, turned and shushed him.

"Staying quiet is always *my* advice," said a voice.

Peter turned. A woman seated at a small table rose and greeted the reporter with a hug. She eyed the four teens. "So these are the Misfits," she said. She crossed her arms as she spoke, and Peter saw in that simple gesture a world of challenge: *Impress me.*

"Misfits, Inc.," corrected Peter. He fumbled for his business cards again and handed her one.

As she read the card, Peter studied the woman. She wore a navy blue business suit, accented by a white blouse and a red silk scarf. Her hair was blond and swept back. Her red fingernail polish shone like the enamel on a new car. Peter quickly put it all together: The woman had to be either a judge or an attorney, and she was way too young to be a judge.

Rebecca went through the introductions. "Peter, Byte, Jake…" She paused. Peter noted the way her upper teeth dug into her lower lip. "…and Mattie," she finally said. "I'd like you to meet Cheryl Atterbury."

The woman shook each of their hands with a strong grip and a quick, businesslike up-and-down. "Rebecca speaks highly of you," she said. "So does Lieutenant Decker over at Robbery Division."

Peter raised an eyebrow. *Decker? The woman's been doing her homework.*

She went on. "But I am not convinced this is a good idea. Really, Rebecca, what do we expect to accomplish?"

Now that he knew the woman had gone so far as to ask Decker about him and his friends, Peter wasn't about to let her just shoo them away. He stepped forward. "I suspect," he said, "that it's not really your call to make, right? You're not the one who wanted us here. Your *client* wants to see us."

The woman's shoulders stiffened a bit. She strode toward a door at the back of the room, opened it, and whispered something to a guard on the other side.

A moment later another woman entered, clad in a bright orange jumpsuit with black numbers stenciled across the front: a county prison uniform. Chains on the prisoner's arms jingled as she walked, and the sound seemed loud and bizarrely cheerful in the silent room. Peter would expect a prisoner to be wearing handcuffs, but these were shackles. A female guard—the same woman who moments ago had been sitting behind the desk up front—guided the woman to one of the folding steel chairs that surrounded the wooden table. She sat, her arms quivering in her lap. Her hair, thin and unwashed, fell across her face. She moved it aside with a flick of her head, revealing pale skin, a nose dotted with freckles, narrow lips, and eyes the color of a swimming pool.

Peter heard a huffing sound, like a child sucking in air after a long cry. He turned and saw that Mattie's eyes were wide, and his skin had gone white.

A faint voice, like fine sandpaper brushing across wood, came from the other side of the room. "Mattie?" it said. The woman in orange was leaning forward.

At the sound of her voice, Mattie's started to tremble. Then it seemed something inside him exploded. He shot across the room, threw open the door, and was gone. His footsteps rang out in the linoleum hallway—loud at first, then softening…softening…until Peter could no longer hear them at all. A distant door slammed. Rebecca Kaidanov placed her hand over her mouth and closed her eyes.

The others stared at the open door and now-empty hallway.

"What was that about?" Jake asked.

"I'll get him," said Byte. She handed her computer bag to Jake and ran after Mattie.

From across the room, the jangling of the woman's chains grew louder. Peter turned to look at her. Her nose, her freckles, her eyes, her face—they all suddenly seemed familiar. Her hands were shaking even more uncontrollably.

"So," Peter said, "you're Mattie's mother."

Byte ran. Mattie wasn't in the outer waiting area, plunking coins in the snack machine. He wasn't in the car. Byte wandered along the rows of cars, but she didn't find Mattie among them. *Probably hiding in that way of his,* she thought. She frowned. Mattie, she knew, had a gift. At four foot eleven, he could pretty much make himself invisible when he wanted to, and though Byte wasn't entirely sure why, this appeared to be one of those times he wanted to.

He wasn't at the gate.

Byte crossed the street to a small convenience store called Zippy-Mart. As she neared it, she was struck by the look of the neighborhood. She knew the downtown, with its antique stores, upscale coffee shops, and frozen yogurt cafés, but she had never visited this area of Bugle Point. This store sat in a gray brick building spattered with swirls of gang graffiti. Yet next to the gang signs was an airbrushed mural of a young Latina clutching a baby wrapped in a blue blanket. Fluffy white clouds hovered over the two, and a golden light streamed through the clouds, bathing her face and the face of her baby. As though this light were too bright even for her, the Latina wore designer sunglasses.

Byte entered the store. A man with a wispy goatee stood behind the counter, his thumbs stabbing at the buttons of a hand-held video game. He didn't bother to look up. Exploring the store, Byte saw hamburgers in yellow foil growing stale beneath a heat lamp, greasy hot dogs rolling on a stainless steel warmer, a machine that spat out blue- and red-colored ice drinks—but no Mattie.

She left, the tiny bell on the door jangling behind her, and leaned against the store's outer wall. The urban Madonna and child painting stared down from above her left shoulder.

Where could Mattie have gone? she wondered.

The next moment Byte heard a sound from behind her—a light, barely audible grunt, like the sound a person might make as he lifted something heavy. She heard the sound again and realized it was coming from around the corner. She turned to look, crinkling her nose at the smell that came from the metal dumpster there. She heard the sound again.

"Hello?" she called.

The noise had come from the other side of the dumpster. Byte took a few tentative steps and found Mattie sitting on the blacktop, his back against the building's wall. In front of Mattie, and in pieces, lay what appeared to be Jake's chromatic tuner. It was a device Jake used—but didn't really need—to tune his clarinet. Mattie had used his Leatherman tool to pry the tuner apart. He was now jabbing a small screwdriver against a screw that held a circuit board in place. He forced the screw into a turn, grunting as he did.

"Mattie," said Byte, "what are you doing?"

The plastic holding the screw in place suddenly broke in Mattie's hand, sending screwdriver, plastic, and circuit board flying in all directions. Mattie gathered the pieces and struggled to fit them together, like a three year old playing with a jigsaw puzzle.

Byte put her hand on his, stopping him. "Talk to me," she said.

Mattie looked at the broken tuner as though he just now recognized it. "This is Jake's," he said. "I…I found it in the car. It helps me calm down to…to take things apart and put them back together."

"I know." Byte sat next to him. "Hey," she said, "what's wrong?"

"That was my mother in there," Mattie said quietly.

Byte drew in a breath. "Oh."

She knew little about her friend's parents, only that Mattie's grandparents had raised him since he was five. What she did know came down to this: In all the time she had known Mattie, Byte could not recall a single moment when he mentioned either of his parents visiting him, calling him, or even sending a card.

"You don't want to go back and hear what she has to say?" Byte asked.

Mattie seemed to come out of his haze. He turned to her, his eyes clear and defiant. "No," he said.

"Okay," said Byte. She scooted closer to him and placed an arm around his shoulder. She had never realized before how thin and bony he was. Byte was very thin herself, but right now she felt that holding Mattie was something like holding a bird in her hand. Mattie's head collapsed against her shoulder, and the two stayed there for several minutes, saying nothing. After a while, his shoulders began to shake, and he put his arms around her. When he finally looked up, his face was red and streaked with tears. Byte thought of going back into the Zippy-Mart for a napkin but she didn't want to leave him. She fished a couple of her eyeglass wipes from her pocket and handed them to him.

Mattie swabbed his face with the flimsy tissues, wadded them into a ball, and stared at them in his hand. "I hate her," he said.

Unsure how to respond, Byte kept quiet.

Mattie hauled himself to his feet, tossed the wipes into the dumpster, and picked up the remains of Jake's tuner. "Come on," he said.

"We're going back?"

Mattie brushed his hands against his jeans. "I'll hate myself if I talk to her," he said, "and I'll hate myself if I don't. So I might as well hate myself and find out what's going on at the same time."

Byte nodded, gripped his hand, and the two of them walked back across the street.

Peter noticed the streaks on Mattie's face the instant he and Byte returned, but he said nothing. Mattie leaned against the wall without so much as a glance at the woman in the prison uniform.

The attorney stared at her notes. "Okay, the facts are as follows: Two days ago the victim, a Mr. Joseph Underwood, aged 67, was struck by a car matching the make—"

"*Allegedly* matching," said Peter.

The woman looked up at him—quite clearly (as opposed to allegedly) annoyed at being corrected by a teenager. "Yes, of course," she said. "*Allegedly* matching the make, model, color, and license number of the car owned by Ms. Marcetti here."

"And the victim?" asked Peter.

"The victim is in critical but stable condition at Mercy General."

The woman in the prison uniform—Mattie's mother, Peter reminded himself—looked up at her lawyer. "I want to testify," she said.

"Carla," said the attorney, "we discussed this. You *can't* testify."

Carla Marcetti shifted in her chair. The chains around her wrists rang like sleigh bells. "But how can I tell the jury my side of the story if you won't let me testify?"

Peter knew what the attorney's answer would be even before she spoke, and he suddenly wished Mattie wasn't in the room to hear it.

"Because of *these*," said Ms. Atterbury. The papers in her hand rattled as she waved them. "If I let you take the stand, the jury will hear about every one of these."

The reporter, Rebecca, nervously fingered the camera dangling from around her neck. "Mattie?" she asked. He said nothing in response. He didn't even look at her.

Peter felt a rush of pity—not for the prisoner, who had made her own choices, but for Mattie. Mattie had not chosen his mother. He had not chosen the life she led. "Carla has priors," Peter said. "Priors" were earlier convictions—crimes Carla Marcetti had committed in the past. Apparently this wasn't the first time she had been in trouble with the law.

The attorney nodded. Mattie, who had turned his back on the conversation, suddenly spun around, and for the first time made full eye contact with the mother he hadn't seen in ten years. As he did, Cheryl Atterbury rattled off a grocery list of Carla's crimes. "Shoplifting. Misdemeanor drug possession. "Shoplifting *again*. Driving under the influence." She released the sheets with a flick of her hand, letting them flutter into her open briefcase. "Frankly, Carla, a jury that hears all this isn't going to care whether you ran over that guy. They're going to think you belong in jail anyway."

"But I'm innocent!" She looked with hope from one Misfit to another, finally settling on Peter. "Will you help me?" she begged. "I've read about you in the newspaper. I know how you've helped people. Maybe you can help me, too. I don't have much money, but I can pay you a little…" She shifted her gaze past Peter. "Mattie?" she said. "Please? I know I'm not…" Her voice trailed off. Mattie had not stopped looking at the woman, and the sheer hatred in that look forced Carla into silence. He moved to the door, gripped the knob for a long moment, then pushed the door open.

This time, his footsteps down the hall were steady and unrelenting, as though he would walk and walk until he reached the edge of the ocean or the end of the world.

Byte watched Mattie as he climbed into Rebecca's Tracker. He struggled with the seat belt, unable to make the metal tongue fit inside the buckle. When it finally snapped in, his shoulders slumped and he leaned his head against the window. Jake, who had once again taken the shotgun seat, turned to Mattie. "You all right?"

Mattie raised his head slowly as though he had just awakened. For a moment it seemed he wasn't sure what he wanted to say. "Oh. Yeah. I broke your tuner," he said. "Sorry. I'll fix it later."

"You broke my…?" Jake apparently decided to let it drop. Mattie again turned his face to the window.

"Okay," said Peter. He was frowning, flipping through a manila folder containing several sheets of paper. Before leaving the jail, he had convinced Cheryl Atterbury to make photocopies of all the police reports and witness statements. He now held in his hand all the evidence against Mattie's mom. Apparently it looked bad. Byte watched as he tapped one of the sheets with his finger. "I want to talk to this Micah Washington kid. He's the one who identified Ms. Marcetti's car. Let's see how sure of himself he is. And his mother—"

"Count me out," said Mattie.

He was still staring through the window, his voice little more than a whisper against the glass, but everyone heard him.

Byte reached over and touched his arm. "Mattie," she said, "she *is* your mother."

Mattie spun around. "Don't talk to me about my mother! I know who my mother is! That…*woman*…at the prison hasn't said a word to me in ten years. She couldn't even pick up a telephone on my birthday." Mattie was shifting, moving from moments of haziness to moments of clarity. "And hasn't it occurred to you that she's probably *guilty*? You can waste your time on her, but I won't."

40 He turned away again. Byte watched as he took one of the Misfits' business cards from his pocket and, with the concentration of a surgeon, tore it into tiny pieces, which he then crumpled in his fist. Byte expected him to open his fist a moment later to reveal that he had magically restored it to one piece. He was always entertaining himself with tricks like that. She smiled, anticipating the outcome, but when Mattie opened his hand, all that remained were the torn pieces. Without looking at them, he turned his hand over and let them fall into his lap.

The remainder of the trip was silent. Byte saw Rebecca Kaidanov glancing in the rearview mirror.

Mattie noticed. "You could have warned me," he said quietly. His head lolled against the window, moving with every turn of the car.

"I'm sorry. It's the only way she'd meet with you, and she needed your help. I'm sorry—"

"Look, you have to drop off Peter and Jake at the school so they can get their cars. You'll be passing by my house on the way."

"I'll drop you off first," said Rebecca.

Twenty minutes later they arrived at Mattie's. Without a word to his friends, he gathered up his backpack with the broken pieces of Jake's tuner clattering inside and pushed the seatback forward. He stepped out, and Byte saw him brush his fingers against the lap of his pants. The torn bits of the business card blew away in the wind.

"I'll talk to you later?" called Byte. Mattie trudged up the brick walkway toward his house. He threw up his hand in a sort of wave. Jake, leaning out the passenger window, stared at their retreating friend.

"Are we doing the right thing by helping this woman?" Byte asked.

Jake shook his head. "I don't know."

"Learning the truth is always the right thing," Peter declared.

"It's not just about the truth, though," said Byte. "It's about Mattie too."

"Well, what if the lady's innocent?" asked Jake. "Do we *not* help her, just because Mattie's upset? I mean, he has a right to be upset, but—"

"*Exactly*," said Peter. "Find the truth, and everything else works out."

Byte stared at Mattie's lowered head and slumped shoulders, his body shadowed by the overhang of the porch until he walked inside.

She wasn't so sure Peter was right.

"Where ya been?"

Mattie's grandmother leaned in the doorway of the kitchen, wiping her hand on a dishtowel. The smell of marinara sauce wafted in from the stovetop. Along with it, Mattie caught the strong scent of meat, onion, and garlic.

He smiled weakly. "Spaghetti and meatballs?"

"Mostacciolli. That's sausage you smell."

Mattie nodded and walked past her, thinking of nothing but collapsing onto his bed and closing his eyes until dinnertime. His grandmother stopped him with a hand on his shoulder. "Hold on, buster." She turned him around, placed hands on *both* his shoulders, and studied him the way she would study the ingredients list in an old family recipe, frowning over every nuance of his expression. Mattie would not complain about being tired or…overwhelmed. Nora Ramiro had little patience with whining. She had grown up in rural Alabama, and in her house the only payback for whining was an extra swat on the rump.

"You all right?" she asked.

"Yeah. Fine."

She studied him a moment longer, and her hands left his shoulders and carefully straightened the collar of his shirt. She looked in his eyes, smiling. "You're in trouble with me, young man. You didn't make your bed today."

"Sorry."

She spun him in the direction of the hallway that led to his bedroom, then gave him a gentle push to get him going. "Put your things away," she said, "and wash your hands. Dinner in fifteen minutes, then homework. I wanna see your assignments when you're finished."

Mattie trudged down the hall. "'Kay, Mamacita."

He could hear her snort. "I'll Mamacita you right on the behind."

When he reached his bedroom, he heard a loud noise, and only then realized he had dropped his heavy backpack to the floor. He stood a moment, staring at the rumpled sheets and blanket on his bed, and then he just tipped over. He fell, air whooshing past his ears, sheets and blanket billowing around him when he hit the bed.

Every muscle and joint of his body ached.

That woman in the jail is not my mother, he told himself. Mothers did not abandon their children. Mothers were something bigger than a biological accident. "Mother," as Mattie understood it, was not a name or title, but a job description: Mothers wiped their hands on kitchen towels and asked you where you had been all afternoon. Mothers jumped on your case for forgetting to make your bed and peeked over your shoulder to see if your homework was done. That woman at the prison was not his mother.

The others could waste their time on her.

He wouldn't.

He hated her.

chapter
three

byte peered through the window in the library door. Though the library was dark, she could see Ms. Langley, the librarian, standing behind the checkout counter. Ms. Langley shoved her purse into some hiding place beneath the counter and turned to a row of toggle switches on the wall behind her. Even from where she stood, Byte could hear the switches—*Chunk! Chunk! Chunk!* And as each one clicked into place, a bank of fluorescent lights in the ceiling hummed to life.

Byte tapped on the window and waved.

Before coming to unlock the door, the librarian reached for a sharpened pencil that lay atop her desk. She tucked it behind one ear, where her hair would keep it in place the entire day. Byte smiled. The pencil-in-the-hair meant Ms. Langley was ready to begin work. The librarian approached the door, waved a hello through the window, and Byte heard a jangling of keys followed by the ratcheting sound of the lock turning.

The door swung open. About six inches. And a librarian—who was decidedly *not* ready to begin work for the day—instantly filled that six-inch gap. "Good morning, Byte," said Ms. Langley. "Have we forgotten that the library doesn't open until 7:30?" Ms. Langley wore an oversized watch with large numerals. She held up her wrist so Byte could see it.

"I know," said Byte, "but I needed a quiet place to talk to Jake, and I was hoping you'd let us in early. Just a few minutes."

The librarian peered at Byte over the rims of her glasses. "And why would Jake come here before the library opens?"

"I told him to."

"So basically," said Ms. Langley, "you told Jake to meet you here—*in* the library, *before* the library opens—even though you hadn't even asked me for permission yet. Have I pretty much got the story right?"

Byte winced. "Last night, when I was justifying it to myself, it sounded better."

The librarian stepped aside and swung the door open. "Five minutes," she said. "Lock the door behind you until Jake comes."

He arrived a few moments later. Byte grabbed his hand and dragged him to a table in the back. "We have to talk," she said. She pushed him into a seat and pulled a chair out for herself across from him. She planted her elbows on the table and laid her chin in her hands. "Mattie wouldn't come to the phone when I called last night."

"I know," said Jake. "I called too."

"And my guess is that he probably won't be coming to school today either."

Jake looked down at the tabletop and fiddled with his

46 notebook. All the Misfits were close, but Jake had made himself sort of a big brother to Mattie. An image from the past came to Byte's mind: Jake, dappled by moonlight, carrying an injured Mattie to safety from a dark forest. Since that time the two boys had been inseparable.

"He'll be all right," Byte said.

Jake nodded.

"In the meantime," Byte went on, "we have another problem."

Jake glanced toward the library door, then back at Byte. "Shouldn't we wait for Peter?"

Byte smiled conspiratorially. "Actually, no," she said. "Peter *is* the problem."

Jake leaned forward, and Byte's voice dropped to a whisper. "Mattie will be all right," she said, "but until he comes around, Misfits, Inc. has only three members."

"So?"

"So…we always break up into pairs to investigate," Byte said. "It's safer, and we have at least two witnesses to every conversation. Two brains working."

"We can all three work together then," said Jake.

"That would take too long," Byte said. "We need two teams. So," she continued, "either we *don't* help Mattie's mom—"

Jake finished the sentence for her. "Or we need another Misfit."

Byte wrapped her arms around her computer bag, waiting.

"But who could we get?" Jake asked.

"Ooooh, I don't know. Someone honest, someone almost as smart as Peter…" suggested Byte. "Maybe even someone we know and like…"

Jake frowned, once again staring at the tabletop. Byte knew he'd put it all together, so she just folded her arms and waited. A moment passed. Then another. Jake's eyes suddenly shot up at her, and his lips slowly peeled back in a smile that looked every bit as devilish as Byte felt. He laughed a quiet *heh heh heh* that sounded like a mad scientist in a really bad sci-fi movie. "Oh, man," he said, "Peter's gonna *hate* this…"

"Which is why he doesn't get to vote," Byte said. She shrugged. "Besides, he won't hate it. He'll *pretend* to hate it. He'll put on a show, but we both know what's really going on, right?"

Jake, still laughing, threw up his hands in a surrender gesture. "Okay, okay," he said, "I'm with you. I just want to be sitting across from Peter when you tell him, because I sure as heck want to see the look on his face. Think someone on the yearbook staff will let us borrow a camera?"

"She'll be perfect!" Byte insisted.

"Hey, I'm not arguing."

Byte threw open the case containing her laptop computer and quickly powered it up. In a moment she was typing a note to the newly invited member of Misfits, Inc. As she hooked the computer to the portable ink-jet printer in her bag, she had to concentrate to make sure the smile on her face didn't appear too triumphant. This new member would certainly keep Peter on his toes, and as an added plus, Jake would have little choice but to hang out with Byte the entire investigation.

I love this plan, she thought.

She folded the note in quarters and stared at the blank paper for a moment. Then she picked up her pen and carefully drew the Misfits' emblem across the front of the note.

"Okay," she said. "Now it's official."

She and Jake gathered their belongings and headed toward the exit. "You know," Jake said, holding the door open for her, "I had no idea you were this evil."

Bugle Point High School lunchroom
Four hours later

"No," said Peter. "No no no no no!" From over his hamburger, he glared at Byte, then at Jake. "I will spell it out for you," he offered. "N-O. I will write it for you—" Here he set his burger down, grabbed his highlighter, ripped a sheet of paper from his notebook, and scribbled the word across it in huge golden letters. He held it up so Byte and Jake could see, then crumpled it and tossed it into a trash can. "And quit smiling," he ordered Byte and Jake. "Nothing funny is happening here."

Around him, the cafeteria buzzed with voices. Lunch period had begun only moments earlier. Dozens of students stood in the serving line, sliding plastic trays across a narrow, stainless steel counter. A few looked in the direction of the commotion Peter had caused.

"It makes sense," said Byte. Her wire-framed granny glasses slipped, and she scrunched up her nose to set them aright. For that instant, Peter thought, she looked a little like a baby rabbit. Oddly enough, she chose that moment to bite down on a carrot stick. It snapped between her teeth as if to say, "So *there*."

Jake, Peter noted, had already finished his cheeseburger and was frowning over a half-eaten Tater Tot. "And I suppose," Peter said, "you also think this ridiculous idea is worth considering."

"Whoooaaa, don't look at me," said Jake. He popped the Tater Tot into his mouth. "I'm just a witness here. Your fight's with her."

"She'll drive me crazy," Peter pleaded.

"She's smart," countered Byte.

"She's been out of touch."

"She knows us," said Byte. "We can trust her."

Peter fumbled for an instant, then finally tossed the hand grenade: "She *lied* to us once."

"She made up for it."

Peter raised his hands. "Yes," he said, "true. But she still can't work with us. We don't even know where she is." He leaned back, locking his hands behind his head.

Byte smiled. "Yes, we do."

"We do?"

"She's back at school today," said Byte. "She e-mailed me a week ago to tell me."

Peter heard his voice climb an octave. "She's here? Today? *Now?*"

"I reminded you of that this morning," said Jake.

Peter pointed a finger at him. "You never said she was *here*."

Jake shrugged. "She is."

"Well, *where is she?*" Peter practically shouted. He stood, planting his fists against the tabletop.

Jake and Byte looked at each other and burst out laughing. Byte tried to say something, but Peter couldn't hear it for the laughter. "What?" he asked. "What?"

Byte pointed just past Peter's left shoulder. "Behind you," was all she could force out. Peter spun around, and his eyes barely had time to focus on a mass of auburn curls. Before he could speak, before he could do anything, a face loomed right in front of his nose, too close to really see. Hands patted either side of his face. "You know, Braddock," said a voice. "Magnet schools aren't all they're cracked up to be. No one there had your brains, so I was forced out of fairness to use only half of mine. No one drove me crazy—well, I take that back, but no one did it as well as you. No one arranged dates where I got shot at. I missed the romance, you know?"

The face then drew apart from him, becoming clearer. Standing before Peter was a girl he once thought he'd never see again: Robin Sutter. Sharp, brassy, pain-in-the-behind Robin Sutter. She folded her arms and studied him with an expression so murky Peter had no idea what it meant. Were those eyes glaring at him? Were those lips smiling? She stood with her weight on one leg, which called Peter's attention to the way her jeans fit around her hips. And to the way her free leg bent slightly at the knee. And to the way he was *really* staring at her.

"Hi," he said.

Robin grinned and wrapped her arms around his neck in a hug. Peter found his arms tightening around her for a moment. With a great effort, he commanded them to hang limply at his side. They obeyed the order, but like soldiers fighting a battle they weren't sure they wanted to win.

Robin, Byte, and Jake chattered so that Peter could hardly keep up. He opted not to try. He heard snippets— Jake relating how he'd acquired his antique clarinet, Byte singing the praises of her new laptop, Robin talk- ing…well, endlessly. Robin blended with their group like someone who had always belonged there, Peter thought. And with that thought came images of Mattie—his entire body quivering, his cheeks huffing as he struggled to breathe. Peter even felt a passing wave of anger: Robin Sutter could not take Mattie's place. Robin Sutter was *not* a Misfit!

Yet she was. Her hand patted his knee, and something like electricity went through him. Based on the way he was wavering, Peter knew he was on the verge of letting his emotions run this show, which made him *extremely* uncomfortable. Emotions were untrustworthy and more than a little dangerous. And frankly, he didn't quite know what to do with them. Robin's voice, right next to his ear, startled him. "So Peter," she said teasingly, "what's your GPA?"

The question had its intended effect: Peter melted—like the bubbly cheese on Mattie's favorite pizza. Of course Robin was a Misfit. Robin had always been a Misfit. He thought back to the last time he had heard her say those words.

"So Peter, what's your GPA?" she asked.

Peter sucked in a deep breath. Should he answer? Since sixth grade, he and Robin Sutter had been like two sprinters tearing toward the same finish line. Peter usually had the higher GPA; Robin made Honor Society. He won last year's chess tournament; she was captain of the debate team. The rivalry continued. Now, at the end of each semester, Peter Braddock and Robin Sutter went to the school's counseling office and requested a peek at their current scores, calculated by computer to the third decimal.

"Let's have it, Peter," said Robin.

"Well... I went up a little. 3.989."

"I don't believe it!" Robin groaned. You're still ahead of me. Mine's 3.987."

Peter shook his head as though the difference didn't matter. "So?" he said. "It's no big deal. Two hundredths of a grade point."

Robin's eyes narrowed. "Two thousandths of a grade point, Braddock. How do you keep your scores up with a math sense like that?"

Now that he was once again in Robin's Sutter's presence, Peter surrendered. More accurately, something like the wall of Jericho crashed inside him, kicking up a sky full of dust and letting him see, finally, what was on the other side. It was this: He and Robin Sutter were too much alike. Bright, competitive, and born with egos that should probably move to Alaska for the extra space. No matter how often Peter thought of Byte, no matter how attracted to Byte he claimed to be, Robin Sutter would be always be a presence niggling at the back of his mind. Peter had a sudden empathy for those ancient people he'd once read about, the ones who drilled holes in their heads to let out unpleasant thoughts.

He took his fries—he had only eaten two of them—and tossed them in the trash. "Okay," he said. "Let's look at what we have." He zipped open his backpack, drawing out the folder of documents the attorney, Cheryl Atterbury, had given him.

"Byte filled me in a little," said Robin. "Is it as bad as it looks?"

"Maybe worse," said Peter. "Carla—Mattie's mom—drives a Chevy Malibu that matches the make, model, color, and license plate number of the car that hit the old man, Mr. Underwood." He flipped through the pages. "The main witness is a ten-year-old kid named Micah Washington. From these papers, he sounds like he knows what he talking about. He's got the model, the license plate number…everything."

"Does she have an alibi?" asked Byte.

Robin helped herself to some of the papers and began leafing through them. Peter glared at her, but she didn't seem to notice.

"It says here," said Robin, "that she claims to have been alone in her apartment, watching TV."

Jake snorted. "Oh, well, there you go. I'm convinced she's innocent now."

"Hey," said Peter. "I wonder if the police are doing forensics on the car. You know, checking any dents, seeing if they match up to where the man was hit."

"No doubt they're trying to," said Robin. "But it's an old car, probably has lots of dents."

Byte slipped the sheet from Robin's hand and studied it. "Hmmm…you're right," she said. "It looks bad. But wait—" Her eyes scanned the page. "She lives in an apartment, right? Someone might have stolen the car without her even knowing."

Jake brightened. "Hey, that's possible!"

Peter shook his head. "It's possible," he told them, "but then we're saying someone stole her car, drove it twenty-seven miles, committed a felony—"

"—and then calmly gave her the car back," finished Robin. "You're right. It doesn't make sense."

Peter peered at Robin over the rims of his glasses. "Please don't finish my sentences for me," he said.

"Sorry," came the reply.

"Because you used to do that—" Peter went on.

"—all the time. I remember," said Robin. Her hand flew to her mouth in a gesture totally lacking in sincerity. *"Oops."*

"Robin," said Byte, "you and Peter should talk to this Micah Washington. Jake and I will go talk to Mrs. Underwood."

Peter had been looking at Robin, but now his head slowly turned in Byte's direction. Did she just lay out a plan? Byte *never* gave orders.

"What?" said Byte. "Did I say something wrong?"

Peter shook his head, but his mind raced. It was just the plan he would have offered up, if Byte hadn't spouted it first. Byte had been thinking about this case, planning an investigation in his absence! And she had partnered him with Robin. This whole morning was turning into one big sucker punch.

"Peter!" called Byte. "Earth to Peter. Snap out of it. All the evidence here says that Carla is guilty. I'd really like to prove it wrong."

Peter reached for the file, tapping its edges against the lunch table to straighten them. Byte was right. Someone needed to speak with Micah Washington. Someone needed to hear the kid tell his story, to get a sense of what he really knew and, most importantly, how convincing he would be in front of a jury. From what Peter gathered, the words that came out of this kid's mouth would either set Mattie's mother free or put her in prison for a very long time.

"Peter?"

The voice seemed to come out of nowhere. Peter blinked and turned toward the sound, almost surprised to see Robin Sutter looking back at him.

"I don't want to be the rain on this little picnic," she

said, "but I've been looking through these files, and, well…" she paused, taking a moment to glance at Peter, Byte, and Jake before continuing. "I think that we have to strongly consider the possibility that Mattie's mother may be…guilty."

Byte looked down at the tabletop and quietly rolled up her canvas lunch bag with its rainbow Apple logo.

"We all understand that," said Peter. "But as long as there's a chance she's innocent, we have to follow every lead—for Mattie's sake. Mattie needs to know."

The new tennis shoes squeaked against the polished marble staircase. Dustin Quaid smiled at the sound. It was like the rubbery squeal of Michael Jordan cutting across a gym floor. He liked, too, the weightless feel of his new hockey jersey, which was not a real hockey jersey at all, but rather a designer's version of one. It draped across Dustin's stooped shoulders and fell to a point just above his knees. Beneath the jersey was a pair of cargo pants. The soft denim legs, almost as wide across as the rims on Dustin's Mustang, bunched around his ankles and brushed against the floor. On his head sat a high-priced ball cap turned backwards, its bill shaped in a deep curve. Dustin had found the clothes in three different shops—four, if he included the gold chains. In each place, he had torn the tags off at the counter and worn the clothes right out the door, carrying his own clothes in snazzy store bags. All his purchases were designer brands, and all expensive—just like Gordon ordered.

Squeak. Squeak. Dustin imagined drumming a basketball against the marble, feeling it slap against his palms. When he reached the top of the staircase, he looked around and knew he was lost. Bugle Point Plaza, the largest mall in the county, was packed with shoppers eager to escape the misty rain outside. Loud noise pounded him from every direction—the wide-screen television at the entrance to Electronics Express, the numbing Muzak from the art gallery, the hip-hop pumping from Footlocker, the clangs and dings from a game arcade called Tilt! He didn't remember seeing these stores on the way in. The restaurant was on the second level, Dustin reminded himself, but *where?* Gordon was waiting, and he would be angry if Dustin were late. The envelopes in his hand suddenly felt wet from his perspiration.

Dustin wasn't winded, but his heart pounded. He needed to find that restaurant! He saw a familiar-looking department store at the end of the long marble walkway and began jogging in that direction, dodging shoppers along the way. Hadn't he seen that store near the restaurant? The squeak of his new shoes turned to a rubbery thudding as he ran even faster. Yes, he remembered Gemstone Books, and Toy World, with its display of ceramic dolls and robotic pets. The restaurant should be right about…

Dustin bent over and breathed deeply from his running. Before him were the potted trees and brass railing that marked the entrance to La Femme de Désir. Gordon said it meant "woman of desire" in French, which is one reason he liked eating there.

When Dustin caught his breath, he entered the restaurant, striding past a male host in black suit and tie. The host, his long nose tipped up like the barrel of a rifle, stared at Dustin as he passed. Dustin glanced at the tables. He saw white tablecloths, heard glasses clinking and silverware clanging against china plates, but he caught only the slightest whisper of conversation.

He continued his sweep of the room. In one corner, seated at a table with a young man dressed quite similarly to Dustin, was Gordon Moxley. Gordon was laughing. *Good,* thought Dustin. *Maybe he hasn't noticed I'm late.* He walked slowly toward the table, his fingers tightening around the damp envelopes.

"Hey, Gordon," said Dustin. "I'm back."

Gordon Moxley's thick, shoulder-length black hair stood in stark contrast to the summery white cotton suit he wore. His collarless shirt, open at the neck, revealed bronzed skin carefully manufactured in a tanning booth. He wore a diamond ring on each hand, which made little lights dance in Dustin's eyes when Gordon was gesturing. Gordon took a sip of wine from a tall, narrow glass, staring at Dustin's new clothes. "Dustin," he said, leaning back in his chair and gesturing to his guest, "you're late."

At this, Dustin felt his shoulders jerk a little under his loose clothing. "Sorry," he said. He held up the envelopes a little higher.

Gordon looked at his guest. "If you'll excuse me a moment." He stood, placed a hand on Dustin's shoulder, and guided him back through the restaurant and out the door. Once outside, he gestured at Dustin's clothing. "Where's your suit?" he asked.

Dustin swallowed. *Suit?*

Gordon's voice grew huskier. "I give you a thousand dollars and tell you to get some nice clothes while I have lunch and talk business," he said evenly, "and you come back like this? You look like, I dunno, the lead singer of some boys' pop band or something."

Dustin felt cold. When Gordon yelled, you knew he was playing with you, but when he talked like this—

"And what's that on your hand?"

Gordon grabbed Dustin's left hand and flipped it over. *Oh, great,* he thought. *I forgot about the ring.* Dustin had used some of the money to buy a gold ring that fit over two fingers. Over the middle finger were the letters *L* and *O*, while over the ring finger were the letters *V* and *E*. Encrusted around the letters were tiny chips of cubic zirconium. Gordon let go of the hand like he was throwing down a piece of trash.

"I'm sorry, Gordon," said Dustin. He heard his voice quaver, which he knew might make Gordon even angrier, but he couldn't help it. "Don't be mad. I didn't know you meant a suit. Honest."

Gordon's face hardened for a moment, but then it relaxed and he began to chuckle. "Don't worry about it," he said. "It's okay. You like the clothes? They feel good on you?"

Dustin nodded.

"Okay, then." He lightly slapped Dustin's cheek, a gesture Dustin took as a sign of friendship, even fatherly love. Gordon then took Dustin's face in his hands, gripping his head, then he slapped him on the cheek a second time. "You're my number one nephew, right? My...apprentice, okay?" Dustin nodded again. Smiling, Gordon reached into the inside breast pocket of his suit and took out a calfskin wallet. He opened it and withdrew a number of bills. "Here, keep the clothes, but take another thousand and get yourself a nice suit. You ruined"—Gordon pronounced it *ruint*—"the first impression, but there're second impressions too. I gave my word that we were the best, so we gotta look like the best, unnerstand? What do we say about Gordon Moxley's promises, huh?"

"You always keep 'em, Gordon."

"Okay. Now whatcha got for me?"

Oh, right. The envelopes. Dustin handed them over, crinkled and moist. The first contained a set of twenty-four 35mm photographs Dustin had taken outside the county jail yesterday. Dustin was a little unclear about why Gordon had sent him there—Gordon only explained himself when he felt he had to—but Dustin knew it had something to do with Carla.

The pictures were of a young woman and four teenagers. The woman was a reporter for the *Courier* named Rebecca Kaidanov; Dustin had learned that much. Gordon had said nothing of the teenagers. Dustin watched now as his boss flipped through the stack, eyeing each of the photos. The first showed a skinny kid, sixteen or seventeen, with short, dark hair and round, owlish glasses. Behind the kid was a girl with curly brown-blond hair, wire-framed granny glasses at the tip of her nose, and what looked like a laptop computer bag hanging from her shoulder.

"Wonder who these kids are," said Gordon.

"There were four of them," said Dustin. Gordon flipped through the rest of the photos. One showed a huge, muscular guy with a buzz-cut. He had his arm around the neck of another kid, a boy who couldn't have been more than five feet tall. The taller boy was scrubbing a knuckle across the smaller boy's head. In another photo, much further down in the stack, the smaller boy was tearing across the parking lot like he'd just seen a roomful of vampires.

Gordon tapped the photo with a finger. "These kids came with the reporter?"

"Yeah. Got any idea who they are, Gordon?"

Gordon shook his head. "Not yet," he said, "but I will. You're gonna be watching them for me."

"They a problem?"

"Maybe," said Gordon. "We'll see. Keep an eye on 'em. I think I might know who one of 'em is. If they show up around the neighborhood, tell Terrell. Tell him to let the boys handle it."

"Sure—sure, Gordon. These kids—they got something to do with Carla?"

"You shut up about Carla!" Gordon glanced up from the photos, slapping the entire stack sharply against his palm. "I told you not to even talk about Carla." Afraid to meet Gordon's gaze, Dustin found a fallen leaf from one of the potted trees and nudged it with the toe of his new tennis shoe. Gordon stuffed the photos back into the envelope and thrust them against Dustin's chest.

"What else you got?"

"I picked up your mail, like you asked," said Dustin. "You got a letter from your mother."

A look Dustin had never seen before passed across Gordon's face. It was a little kid's look, a Christmas morning smile. "My—my mother?" he asked.

Dustin handed over the envelope. Gordon tore it open, shredding it in his hurry to get to the note inside. It was pastel pink, and folded within it was another slip of paper that Dustin recognized as one of Gordon's personal checks. The amount on the check, Dustin saw, was ten thousand dollars. Gordon read the note, still smiling, but then the paper began rattling in his hand. Gordon's cheeks reddened, and a snarl escaped his throat before he caught himself and swallowed it. Then, in a move so sudden it made Dustin flinch, Gordon tore the check in half. He kept tearing until it was reduced to a handful of tiny bits. When he flung his arms, snowflakes of paper rose into the air and drifted to the mall floor. The letter itself became a pink wad in Gordon's fist. He spun around and slammed his fist into the stone wall that marked the entrance to the restaurant. Turning to Dustin, he opened his hand, and the pink wad fell to the floor. The knuckles of the hand were scraped and red.

Gordon drew several deep breaths and slipped the handkerchief from his coat pocket. It had been there for decoration, Dustin knew, but now Gordon wrapped it around his raw knuckles. With a final glare at Dustin—*do not ask me about this!*—Gordon turned away and walked back into the restaurant to finish his business.

A full minute later, when he was certain Gordon couldn't see him, Dustin bent down and picked up the wad of paper. He tugged at it with his fingernails, peeling it open and smoothing it so he could read the note written there.

Only four words, scrawled in a ragged but feminine hand:

Keep your blood money, it said.

chapter
four

Peter guided his cherry red 1967 Volkswagen convertible down Eighth Avenue. In the passenger seat next to him sat Robin Sutter. Robin had spoken little during the trip, but now she leaned forward to take control of the radio dial. Peter always set the dial to the talk radio station he liked, where news came on every half hour and chattering DJs talked politics with ill-informed people who phoned in. His passenger punched a selector button, setting the radio to a pop station. A woman sang high, trilling notes over a hip-hop beat. Robin smiled at Peter, nodding her head in time to the music. Peter leaned forward and punched a different button. Talk radio again. "Rules of the road," he said. "Everyone knows the driver of the car has total say over the radio." Robin hit the selector button again. A twang of country. The two continued this way, jabbing their fingers at the radio until Robin burst out laughing and Peter finally got the point.

"You don't really care about the radio station, do you?" he muttered.

"No," she said, "but it's tons of fun bugging you."

"Hmph," said Peter.

He knew that the area around the county jail would be full of vacant lots and rundown buildings covered with graffiti, but it had never occurred to him that people also lived around here. Now he saw that this section of Eighth Avenue was lined with squat apartment buildings made of brownstone. Each building stood three stories tall, with a rusty fire escape clinging to one side as though some giant child had gone crazy with an erector set.

"Low-rent, government housing," said Peter.

Robin nodded. "The projects."

Another building—for lack of a better word—grabbed Peter's attention. On a plot of flattened, gray dirt was a seven-story structure made of rusting steel girders and sheets of plywood. The girders stretched into the sky, forming the building's legs and spine. The plywood served as flooring where construction workers could stand.

"The Skeleton Building," Peter said.

"Hmm?"

He pointed at the structure. "I've heard about this. A few months ago, some guy tried to put in a high-end apartment building. He was hoping to build up the whole area, fix up everything. Only some of his investors backed out at the last minute and took their money with them. This was as far as he got. People call it the Skeleton Building."

At the end of the street was a convenience market with steel bars bolted over the windows. Children and older teens gathered in small groups on the street, a few eyeing Peter's car as he passed. One kid's face was swollen, his jaw bruised to the color of blueberries. An old man with an unshaven face lay sprawled at the entrance to one building, his eyes closed. A little boy was rummaging through his pockets for loose change. This neighborhood was nothing like the world Peter knew. Robin must have felt it too. Her voice was quiet as she spoke, and the teasing tone—which was almost always present—had vanished. "There it is," she said, pointing. "119 Eighth Avenue."

Peter pulled up to the curb and parked. The churning inside him grew. He imagined returning to his precious Beetle to find a smashed windshield, torn top, or missing tires. A road crew was filling potholes just half a block ahead, so he put his car in gear again and parked closer to them. He and Robin stepped out and walked—hurriedly—toward the building where the accident had happened. Near the entrance to the building was a wooden sign on which the words "Get Well Joseph" were scrawled in permanent marker. Strewn around the sign were scattered bunches of flowers.

A gate barred the entrance to the building. Peter tried turning the knob, but it was locked. Robin walked over to some mailboxes mounted on the outside wall of the building. Above each mailbox was a plaque bearing a black button, a small speaker, and a slip of paper on which the manager had written the resident's name. Robin found the box that said "Apt. 210, Washington, C." and pushed it. A woman's voice issued from the scratchy speaker. "Yeah? Who is it?"

"Ms. Washington?" said Robin. "May my friend and I come up? We'd like to ask you and your son a couple of questions about the accident you witnessed."

"I already talked to the police."

"We're not the police," said Robin.

The speaker crackled. "Then go away."

Peter started to reach for the button, but he paused when he realized he hadn't a clue what he would say to the woman. He didn't give up easily. Peter hated to lose—in chess, in backgammon, in life in general. He knew he could probably find a way to get beyond this locked gate. Yet he also knew there would be another locked door at the entrance to Corie Washington's apartment, and another guarding every word that came from her mouth. Yes, he could put in a tremendous effort, and he might even make progress, but in the end Corie Washington didn't know him, didn't seem to want to know him, and had no reason for wanting to help. His arm dropped away from the button.

"Come on," he said to Robin. "Let's go."

Before Robin could protest, they heard the sound of footsteps crunching on gravel behind them. As Peter and Robin turned to leave, they saw a group of kids blocking the sidewalk ahead of them. Some of the group seemed as young as seven or eight. A couple of guys looked to be in their twenties. They all moved forward, cutting Peter and Robin off from the car. As the younger ones waited, silent, one of the older members of the group stepped forward.

"This ain't your neighborhood," he said flatly. "What're you doin' here?"

As he and the young man faced each other, Peter felt Robin's hand grip the back of his shirt, crumpling the fabric in her fist. The threat in the man's voice was enough to make Peter stand still, straighten his shoulders, and remain silent. The man was thin and narrow-shouldered, but the tank top he wore revealed tight, rounded biceps and muscular forearms. His fingers were thick and scuffed with patches of white where the skin was rubbed raw.

"We were just leaving," Peter said. He started around the young man, but the man moved with him. Peter stepped back, his forearm hairs tingling.

"You still ain't answered my question," said the young man.

Peter let his mind race, searching for *anything*, any detail about the man that might suggest a way to change the direction this conversation was headed. What flashed to mind were the scuff marks on the man's hands. *What could cause that?* Peter wondered. *It's like he's been handling rocks, or—*

"Cement," Peter said. It took him a moment to realize he had spoken aloud. Both Robin and the young man stared at him, so he pointed to the man's fingers. "You work construction, I bet. You pour cement, right?"

Taken off guard, the man tilted his head back slightly. "I lay brick."

"Really?" said Peter. "That takes skill. My dad just tried to lay down a brick planter all by himself. He said it was the hardest work he'd ever done. It was supposed to be a circle, but it turned out looking like, I don't know, a really bad stop sign." Peter thought he saw the corners of the man's mouth tick upward.

Peter chanced stepping forward, offering his hand. "I'm Peter," he said. "This is my friend, Robin."

The man hesitated, then clasped Peter's hand with his own. The handshake hurt. The man's fingers were incredibly strong. "Name's Jerome," he said.

"Hi," said Peter. From behind him, Robin waved a hello. "We were hoping to talk to Ms. Washington about the accident that injured Mr. Underwood," Peter explained. "We wanted to know if we could do something to help."

"You trying to help old Joseph?" the man asked. Two members of the group looked at each other.

"If we can," said Robin.

Jerome thought for a few moments, then stepped over to the mailboxes. As Peter had done, he pushed the button over Corie Washington's name. The speaker hummed, and the woman's voice once again crackled from it. "I said leave me alone!"

"Hey, Corie," said Jerome. "It's me." He gave Peter and Robin one last appraising stare. "I've been talking to these two, and—well, I think they're all right. They want to help old Joseph. Maybe you should talk to them."

No response. Another long moment passed, and Peter thought Corie Washington had walked away from the speaker in her apartment. But then a buzzer sounded from the gate. An electronic signal unlocked the door.

"Thank you," said Peter.

Jerome nodded.

Peter twisted the knob, opened it, and gestured Robin through the gate.

"Such a gentleman," she said.

"Not really," whispered Peter. "I just want you in front in case someone tries to shoot at us."

The stairs were concrete, lit by yellow lamps that hummed and flickered. Peter and Robin's footsteps echoed off the brick walls, and in the enclosed space the sound seemed hollow and ghostly. From the second floor landing, Peter could see down a hallway lined with apartment doors. Near the end of the hallway two little girls screamed, playing tug-o-war with a doll.

"If I'm following the numbers right," said Robin, "her apartment should be the third one on the left."

It was. As Peter knocked on the door, he could hear a blaring television, the sharp giggle of a little girl, and a woman's voice barking orders. The sense he got was one of general commotion, so when no one answered right away, he knocked again.

The door swung open. Peter found himself staring into the face of a woman who was probably in her late twenties. She had short hair and large, pretty eyes, but the skin beneath those eyes appeared puffy and a little darker in color. The woman needed more sleep, Peter decided.

"Come on in," said Corie Washington. From her tone, Peter understood the rest of the sentence to be *if you must*. She swung the door wide then turned and moved back into the apartment. Peter and Robin followed.

As Peter shut the door behind them, he spied a little girl with pigtails toddling across the floor, grinning and holding one arm high in the air. A sliver of green extended above her closed fist. Corie lunged like a linebacker at the girl. "Tanaya!" she shouted. She pried the girl's fingers apart and snatched something from her hand. Peter realized then it was a jalapeno pepper. "How many times, Tanaya, have I told you not to take things from the fridge without asking?" She turned the little girl's hand over and gave it a quick smack with two fingers. Tanaya wailed. The woman, sighing, hoisted her into her arms. "Sweetie," she said, "what happened the last time you ate one of mommy's jalapenos?"

The little girl's face was flushed, and her cheeks huffed in and out. In a tiny voice she said, "It burnt my mouth."

"Good," said Corie. "You remember." She kissed Tanaya on the cheek and let her slip to the floor. "Go tell Micah I said to let you watch *The Little Mermaid*." She then turned to Peter and Robin. "Go ahead and ask your questions."

She was wearing black polyester pants and a white blouse. As she spoke, she tied on a red-and-white checked apron. The top of the apron had a frilly bib with a plastic tag that read "Snappy's Pizza." Beneath that, spelled out on red label-maker tape, were the words "Corie. Shift Leader." While Robin was explaining to Ms. Washington that they were friends of a reporter who hoped to do a human interest story on Mr. Underwood, Peter began to survey the apartment. It was a large square room, with one section set apart as a tiny kitchen. Nearby sat a vinyl-topped card table with four folding chairs. The "living area" consisted of a television set and an old recliner that rested at a slight but noticeable tilt. Behind it sat a full-sized mattress on a steel frame. Someone, he noted, had made the bed with care, stretching the blanket taut and folding the sheet over nicely. A second mattress, this one twin-sized, lay on the floor next to it.

"Thanks for seeing us, Ms. Washington," said Peter. "We understand you're busy, so we'll try not to take too much of your time."

The woman was scurrying here and there in search of something. "Great. I don't have much time to give you." She picked up a jacket from the floor, snatching a small purse that was hidden beneath it.

"When the accident occurred, you didn't happen to get a glimpse of the driver, did you?" Peter asked.

The woman snorted. "Are you kidding? I was terrified."

From behind him, Peter heard Robin's voice. "Is that Micah over there?" she asked. "He's the one who identified the car that hit Mr. Underwood, right?"

A young boy appeared from behind the recliner. The girl, Tanaya, yanked at his sleeve, and he reached for a videotape that lay atop a VCR and fed it in. A moment later Peter heard Disney theme music.

"Micah," called Corie, "these people would like to talk to you."

Micah made his way over, his feet *galumphing* in shoes that were a little too large and whose laces were undone. A T-shirt advertising a Porsche Boxster draped over the boy's cargo shorts. "Hi, Micah," said Robin.

The boy looked down at the floor, slipping his left foot in and out of its shoe. "Hi."

"Cool shirt," said Peter. "I saw a Boxster for the first time just last week."

"They're fast," said Micah. "They have 217 horses under the hood at 6,400 on the tach."

Peter grinned. "I have no idea what that means," he said.

"I hope it's all right if we ask you some questions," said Robin. "You saw the accident from that window over there?"

Micah nodded. "It was an '82 Chevy Malibu. Blue. The license number was 1XGP394."

"Wow, you're really observant." said Robin. "That's amazing."

"Yeah, you must know a lot about cars," said Peter. "I mean, in just a few seconds you recognized the car and memorized the license plate number. I'm impressed."

Peter prided himself in his ability to observe. But he had nurtured this skill, practiced it, while this ten-year-old boy had in a few instants noticed every detail of Carla Marcetti's car. *Allegedly,* Peter had to remind himself, *allegedly Carla Marcetti's car.* He and Robin had come here to discover exactly how certain Micah Washington was in his observations. When Mattie's mother went to trial, would the boy fall apart, or would he be the witness that sent her to prison?

The boy brightened, "Oh, I *like* cars." He grinned and motioned for them to come with him. "Lemme show you."

Micah led Peter and Robin to a small shelf unit that held several plastic model cars—nine, to be exact, Peter noted. Micah picked one up, a Corvette convertible, and took great delight in spinning its wheels.

"Is that a '63?" asked Peter.

"'61," said Micah soberly. "With scoops on the sides." He returned the model to the shelf, setting it down and adjusting it once…twice…as though arranging a museum piece.

"I guess you knew the Corvette was a '61," Peter suggested, a hint of challenge in his voice, "because it said so on the box."

Micah heard the challenge. He swung around, his grin even wider, and kicked off his loose-fitting sneakers. He ran to the window. Peter and Robin followed, watching the boy and remaining silent. Without prompting, Micah began pointing to the cars below as they traveled along Eighth Avenue. "'99 Chevy Blazer," he announced, "1CFZ870. 2000 Ford F150 pickup, 1DJH587. '68…no, '69 AMC Gremlin." He turned to Peter. "You know, that's about the ugliest car anybody ever built."

Peter pointed. "Try that one," he said.

"That's easy," replied Micah. "'67 Volkswagen Beetle convertible, and the license number is…" He squinted. "It says MISFITS1."

Peter smiled.

"Hey, is that your car? What's Misfits mean?"

Peter sighed. "A misfit," he said, "is someone who's about to go home. Thanks, Micah. I think you've pretty much told us everything we need to know." He motioned to Robin, mouthing the words *Come on.* Corie Washington was scuttling around the tiny kitchen, spooning Hamburger Helper onto plates and throwing desperate glances at her watch. *Waiting for a babysitter,* Peter thought, *so she can get to work.* "Thanks again, Ms. Washington," he called.

Without looking up, the woman waved good-bye with a large spoon.

Robin closed the apartment door behind them. "What do you think?" she asked.

Peter took her elbow and hurried her toward the stairs. "What do I think?" he repeated. "I think Mattie's mother is going to jail for a really long time."

Jake pulled his Ford Escort onto a little nub of a road that ended in a sharp cul-de-sac. Most of the homes here were one- or two-bedroom clapboard affairs with peeling paint and rickety fences.

"There?" he asked, nodding to one on the left.

Byte squinted over the slip of paper in her hands. Carla Marcetti's attorney, Jake recalled, had said the wife of

Joseph Underwood was staying on West Lowell. The house belonged to Mrs. Underwood's sister, and conveniently it was only ten minutes away from the hospital where Mr. Underwood was recovering from surgery.

"That's the one," Byte said.

Jake turned his car into the driveway, feeling the tires thump against a deep rut in the asphalt. As he stepped out of his car, he noted a brick planter just off the crooked porch. Within the planter was a burst of brightly colored flowers—red, yellow, violet, orange— exotic-looking varieties Jake didn't recognize.

"What are those?" he said.

"I don't know," Byte replied. "But they're beautiful, aren't they? Someone spends a lot of time taking care of them." The porch creaked under the weight of their footsteps. Jake pulled open a screen door and knocked on the wooden door behind it. It opened, then made a chunking sound as a brass security chain pulled tight. An elderly woman peered out, her hand gripping the door. Jake glimpsed calluses on the fingers—no doubt from gardening—before the hand withdrew.

"Yes?" The clear, strong voice surprised him.

"Mrs. Underwood?"

"She's inside. Can I help you?"

Byte wrestled with the case that held her computer bag. She unzipped an outer pocket, withdrew a Misfits business card, and fed it through the opening in the doorway.

"She's expecting us," Byte said.

The door closed, the chain rattled, and a moment later the door opened again. The woman swung it wide, and with a flat, expressionless face, gestured the teens in. "Myra," she called, "your visitors are here." She led them through a living room that held a simple armchair and a plush, floral-patterned couch that looked so comfortable, Jake thought, a person might happily sleep on it. An old brass lamp with a fringed shade stood next to the couch. A collection of glass and ceramic giraffes sat on the mantle over the fireplace.

Beyond the living room Jake could see a small kitchen, most of which was taken up by a 1950s-era kitchen table and four vinyl-covered chairs. Seated in one of the chairs was a woman who, in poor light, could have been the twin of the woman who had answered the door. Myra Underwood looked to be in her late sixties. Her hair was graying, her figure plump in a way that suggested a woman who felt both safe and content in her life. She held a paperback book splayed open in her hands, the cover of which showed a muscular pirate in a shirt with poofy sleeves. The title was *My Pirate Love*.

"Myra," said the woman who had brought them in, "why are you reading in the kitchen instead of the living room?"

"Light's better in here." She looked up at Jake and Byte through thick glasses, which she held in place with, of all things, one of those neoprene eyeglass straps favored by beach kids and players of pickup basketball. She tossed the book to the table. "Don't know why I bother. Can't concentrate on the silly thing anyway."

"You know why," said Mrs. Underwood's sister. "You were in that depressing hospital all last night and all this morning. You need a break, some distraction. You also need to eat. Now quit fussing; I'll take you back to the hospital in a couple of hours." She took a Tupperware container out of the refrigerator and spooned something into a bowl, then placed it in a microwave oven.

Myra Underwood turned to Byte. "You must be Eugenia," she said. Her voice was older and cracked a bit more than her sister's, but Jake was unsure whether the difference was age or weariness.

"Yes, ma'am," said Byte. "This is my friend, Jake."

"Sit, please," said Mrs. Underwood. She indicated two of the vinyl chairs. When Byte and Jake sat, she leaned back, slipping her glasses off and letting them dangle by the strap. She looked at the two of them as though measuring up new players at a poker table. Indeed, Jake could imagine this woman playing a mean hand of poker. It wouldn't surprise him to learn she kept a flask of whiskey in her purse or a box of cigars in the kitchen drawer.

"So," she said, "why don't you tell me what makes you so all-fired interested in Joe's accident?"

"Hmph!" snorted the sister. The microwave beeped, and she removed the container, banging it down on the counter.

Jake and Byte had known this question was coming, and both had agreed that it might not be the best

approach to tell Mrs. Underwood the complete truth—
at least for now. How would she react, after all, if she
were to learn that the Misfits were looking for a way to
prove the innocence of the woman who, by all appear-
ances, had struck down her husband?

"We have a friend in the police department," Byte said.
"Lieutenant Marvin Decker. I mentioned him when—"

"Yes," said the woman, "I spoke to your friend the lieutenant. He said you weren't helping him on a case now."
Her eyes flickered back and forth, from Byte to Jake to
Byte again. When neither of them spoke, she folded her
hands and leaned forward. "But he said you were trust-
worthy. He also said you were more honest than sensi-
ble, whatever that means. So what's your question?"

"According to the report," Jake said, "you weren't a witness to the accident."

"Hmph," said the sister again. She let a cupboard door
slam shut.

"Now, Monique," said Mrs. Underwood, "why don't
you just quit all your hemming and hawing and banging
around and say what's on your mind?"

Monique came over to the table bearing a plastic serving tray. On the tray were two cups of coffee, a bowl of
thick, beefy soup, some carrot sticks, and a slice of but-
tered bread. "You know what's on my mind, Myra," she
muttered. She set the tray down in front of her sister and
took one mug of coffee for herself.

Mrs. Underwood turned once again to Jake and Byte.
"Don't mean to be rude," she said. "Would you like some
soda pop or something? We have some Oreos…"

"We're fine," said Jake.

Monique ignored the interruption and went right on with her thought. "You know darn well that wasn't no accident, Myra."

"I don't *know* that," said Mrs. Underwood.

"Well, girl, you better open your eyes." Monique jabbed a finger in Mrs. Underwood's direction. "You'll be next, I'm telling you."

Under the table, Jake felt Byte's toe poke him in the ankle.

"What do you mean it wasn't an accident?" Byte asked.

Monique leaned forward, and her voice dropped to a ragged whisper. "You ever been to Myra's neighborhood?" she asked. "It's terrible. High school kids selling hard drugs on the corner. Gang graffiti all over the buildings. Strange cars coming down the street in the middle of the night, stopping when some shadow steps out from an alley, then moving on. Guns going off, what, a couple times a week?" She looked at her sister for confirmation, but Myra Underwood remained silent. "Old Joe didn't stand for none of that. When the police came, it was because Joe called 'em. If some gangsters got arrested for selling drugs or for carrying guns, it was Joe who identified 'em. The gang in that neighborhood had it in for old Joe Underwood, I'm telling you that!"

"Mrs. Underwood," said Byte, "is that true?"

The old woman nodded. She leaned her head against her sister's shoulder and blew her nose into a napkin. "Monique and I tried to talk Joe into moving in here so

the three of us could take care of each other, but he
wouldn't. He said if we left, there'd be no one to watch
over the neighborhood. 'And what would happen to the
good people who lived there?' That's how he put it.
'What would happen to them?'"

Jake shook his head. Something didn't make sense.
"The police report didn't mention anything about that."

"I told them," said Mrs. Underwood, "but when they
arrested that woman, I think they just dropped everything else. It was an accident, pure and simple. Nothing
to do with gangs."

Monique stood and leaned over the table. "You want to
know who wanted Joe Underwood hurt?" she snapped.
"You just talk to Terrell Briggs. He's the leader of the
gang. He'll know. You talk to *him*."

Myra Underwood squeezed her sister's hand. "Oh
Lord, Monique," she whispered, "don't tell them that.
They're just kids. You'll get them killed."

chapter
five

"much as I hate to admit it, I'm ready to give up," said Peter. At lunchtime, the Bugle Point High School quad was all motion, sound, and color. Conversation among hundreds of students created a loud buzz that served as constant background noise. Shirtless boys played basketball on the blacktop, the metal backboard humming with every goal. Cheerleaders barked out a practice routine. Music blasted from a boom box. Peter had walked past it all and found a distant place on the grassy field.

Robin sat next to him, quietly tearing off bits of crust from her hamburger bun and nibbling at them. "Yeah," she said.

Peter watched Jake walk past a group of students and head toward them, brown bag and fountain drink in his hands. Mike Gilbert, one of the football players who had bothered Peter and Jake the other day, stuck out a leg to trip Jake as he passed. Peter shook his head. *Stupid stupid stupid.* Didn't Gilbert realize—?

"Yeeeeoow!"

The football player's scream echoed very nicely, Peter thought. He felt no sympathy for him. Simply noting Jake's size should have told Gilbert that Jake would just plow right over the leg as though it were a Popsicle stick instead of bone. The football player was gripping his knee and howling. Jake shrugged, said something to the boy and moved on.

"What did you say to him?" Peter asked.

Jake set his lunch bag on the grass and reached in for a french fry. "I said 'Excuse me.'" He looked around. "Where's Byte?"

Robin pointed. "Coming."

Byte was scrambling across the blacktop, clutching her computer bag in one hand and her canvas lunch bag in the other. When she got to them she sat, breath huffing from her. From out of the depths of the bag came a pita bread sandwich wrapped in wax paper, blue corn tortilla chips, a banana, and an eight-ounce bottle of Organic Orchard apple juice. Peter watched the flurry of her hands, heard the rattle of the wax paper, and in two seconds one fourth of Byte's sandwich had vanished.

Then she looked up. Her chewing slowed. She swallowed. "What's everyone staring at?" she asked. "I'm hungry, okay? Get over it."

Jake frowned and peered at her sandwich. "Are you eating *cat food?*"

Byte glanced down at her pita bread. "That's hummus!" she exclaimed. "It's made with ground-up garbanzo beans and sesame paste…and stuff. It's very healthy." Peter thought she came dangerously close to shouting. She looked at him now, clearly expecting him to come to her defense.

"Pita bread I can handle," he said. "You lost me with the hummus."

"Robin, save me," said Byte.

Robin offered a sympathetic smile. "Sorry," she said. "I'm with Peter. Hummus sounds like something you spread on the ground to make the grass greener."

Byte threw up her hands. "Okay. If you're through critiquing my sandwich, I'm going to eat my chips now. Somebody tell me what they found out yesterday."

Peter glanced at Robin and felt a pall of failure. "Nothing helpful," he said. "We talked to Micah Washington. He comes across as a nice kid, and he really sounds like he knows his stuff. A jury's going to believe him."

"We also tried to talk to some other residents in the building," added Robin, "to see what they might know." She held up her fingers and began ticking off their experiences. "Let's see, we had four doors slammed in our faces, five 'I don't know anythings,' two offers to buy drugs, and one guy who actually poked a gun barrel at us through the open doorway." She patted Peter's arm. "But that's okay, because Peter was standing right *behind* me."

"I was covering your back," Peter said.

"*Riiight.* In all fairness, though," said Robin, "I don't think the guy really would have shot us. I think he just planned to, you know, wing us or something." She reached over and slugged Peter in the shoulder.

Jake held a double cheeseburger inches from his mouth, pausing as Robin spoke. "I don't think we can match that," he said.

"We did, however," said Byte, "learn that the accident might not have been so accidental." She explained how she and Jake had spoken with Mrs. Underwood and her sister—and about Mr. Underwood's attempts to rid the neighborhood of its gang element. "She even gave us a name." She pulled out her laptop and powered it up right there on the grass. "Terrell Briggs. I found him in the *Courier*'s morgue."

A newspaper's "morgue" was the place where old stories remained on file. In the case of the *Bugle Point Courier*, the morgue was a vast library reporters could access by computer. Byte had Rebecca's pass code. She clicked her mouse, and her monitor filled with a newspaper story dated six months ago. Centered within the article was a photo of a young black man in handcuffs. "Meet Terrell Briggs."

Peter scanned the article. "Drugs and guns," he said.

"So Mr. Underwood was a pain in Terrell Briggs's behind?" asked Robin.

"That's the least of it," said Jake. "The police arrested several members of Terrell's gang directly because of leads that came from Mr. Underwood." He bit into his burger.

Peter tapped his finger against his chin. What did it all mean? It was incomprehensible that Micah Washington could be so flat-out wrong. He really knew cars. He had demonstrated that far beyond Peter's expectations. His description of that evening's events was confident and detailed. The accident seemed to be nothing more than it appeared—an accident. But now it was clear someone had a *motive* for wanting to hurt Joseph Underwood. Could the truth, then, be even worse than an accidental hit and run? Could Terrell Briggs have gotten Carla Marcetti to hit Mr. Underwood? Peter could tell from the others' silence that they, too, were asking the same question. "We have to go back to Eighth Avenue," he said quietly. "We have to find out more about this Terrell Briggs."

Jake plucked at the grass, holding torn strands of it in his open palm and watching as the breeze took them. "From what I'm hearing," he said, "that neighborhood doesn't exactly sound like the local arcade. How, exactly, do you plan on getting us out of there with the same number of body parts we had when we went in?"

"Robin and I managed it," said Peter. He forced out his most confident and authoritative voice, though even as he spoke, he knew he wasn't being totally honest.

Robin filled in the rest of his thought. "But we just went to one apartment building," she reminded him. "Wandering around there at night could be dangerous."

"So do you have a plan?" asked Jake.

Peter ran his hand through his hair, brushing away the single lock that kept falling in front of his eyes. "No, I don't," he said. While he pondered, his tongue made a clicking sound against the roof of his mouth. "We could talk to Jerome. Maybe he knows something."

"Who's Jerome?" Byte asked.

Peter answered before Robin had a chance to jump in with unnecessary details. "He's this guy we met in front of the apartment building. He helped us get in to see Ms. Washington."

Peter had only half a plan, and half a plan, he knew, was often worse than no plan at all. He considered other options, rejecting them as being equally lame or even lamer than the one he had suggested. As he thought, Peter followed Jake's example, pulling out a handful of grass and holding it to the wind. The grass didn't stir. The breeze had died. Peter, happy to be holding onto something he *could* control, hurled the grass into the air and watched it flutter away.

No one spoke for a very long time. The bell ending lunch rang, and they gathered up their belongings.

"Hey," said Byte, "anyone heard from Mattie?"

It was strange not seeing the others yesterday, Mattie thought. Strange, he realized, until it became clear to him that he had been the one hiding. Peter, Jake, and Byte had likely gone to the usual places—the library in the morning, the quad at break and at noon. Mattie had managed to avoid each place. The talents he had for finding his friends—the eel-like way he slid through crowded halls, the internal radar that told him where they were—he was now using to stay away from them.

The bell rang ending fifth period, startling him. Mattie

scooped up his backpack and was in the hallway before anyone else even reached the door. Other classrooms opened, the hallway filled, and someone bumped Mattie, spinning him around and passing him without a word.

He wondered, briefly, if he was angry with the others. He considered the possibility and decided he was not. The Misfits were only trying to help Carla Marcetti—he still couldn't call the woman "mom"—and maybe they were trying to help him as well. So why was he hiding? Mattie could figure only this: If it took a day and a half for him to realize he was running from them, it would take at least that long to work out why.

At a bank of lockers up ahead he saw Heather Connelly, the girl from his English class. She leaned her head and one shoulder against the lockers. Her fingers slowly spun the combination dial in a way that suggested she didn't much care what number it landed on.

Mattie walked over. "Hi."

"Hi." She tugged on the latch. The locker refused to open. Without comment, she began spinning the dial again.

Mattie made a circular motion with his finger. "You have to shoot past the first number a couple of times before it'll work," he said.

"Uh huh. Am I wearing a sign that says 'Idiot—Please help me'?"

The locker popped open. Heather dumped a couple of books inside and reached for a gym bag. In a moment, she would slam the door shut and walk off, and right now Mattie felt like talking with someone—anyone—as long as the subject wasn't Carla Marcetti.

"Boy or girl?" he asked.

Bang! The locker slam was louder than Mattie had expected. He flinched. Heather Connelly's face drew within a nose-length of his. "*What?*"

Mattie tried to step backward, but the tail of his jacket had gotten caught in her locker door. He yanked once, twice, but it held. "Your kid," he said. "You never told me."

"*Oh.* Sorry. I thought you were making a crack, like maybe I was…" Her voice trailed off. "Never mind."

She twirled the dial again, this time with the speed of a locksmith. In an instant the locker was open, incidentally freeing Mattie, and a wallet appeared in Heather's hand. From within the wallet came a photograph of a blond-haired baby. Mattie couldn't tell much by the photo, but he assumed it was a boy. He wore a yellow shirt with red overalls and sat on a blue carpet, a set of oversized alphabet blocks stacked around him. The scene could have been an infant's nursery, but the blocks were stacked so artfully it had to have been a professional photographer's studio.

"Tyler Madison Connelly," she announced.

"His middle name is Madison?" asked Mattie.

Heather scrunched up her face. "Yeah, it's my mom's maiden name, and Grandma was putting major pressure on me."

Mattie handed her the photo, and Heather started to slip it back into the wallet. Before she did, however, she paused a moment to study it. "He's almost nine months old now." Her face broadened into a smile that made her look very familiar to him. Then he realized why: With that pure, unaffected smile on her face, Heather Connelly looked just the way she had looked in middle school. She reminded Mattie of the girl she used to be.

But then the smile faded. A light left her face. She wore the same vacant and hard look she'd had when Mattie first approached her. She squeezed her eyes shut, and when she opened them again she was crying. No sound. A single tear. It was the tear of a person who couldn't really afford to cry, Mattie thought—a person who didn't have time to cry. She wiped a finger across her cheek, sniffled once, then stuck the wallet and photo back into her locker.

Mattie clapped his hands together just for something to do. "So," he said, "how 'bout that basketball game the other night?"

Heather looked at him, blinking dully.

Mattie shook his head. "No—I mean, what's going on? How are your classes? What...what's your favorite class?" He stammered, searching for the elusive safe question. His hand fumbled in his coat pocket for a roll of hard candy. "Wanna LifeSaver?" he asked.

"Mattie..."

"What?" he said. "What's wrong?"

Heather slumped against her locker. Several students drifted by on their way to the last class of the day. A loud bark of laughter came from down the hall. A paper air-plane flew past. Her eyes sought the floor, much like the way they had when she'd burst into class late. "My boyfriend—Tyler's dad—hasn't called me in a week," she said. "I think he's gonna dump me, and I think I'm gonna have to do this parent thing all by myself, and I am so scared I can feel it in my teeth. That's how I am."

Just then the tardy bell rang. They were late to class. Heather ran off and Mattie found himself alone, staring at the bank of lockers. His mother had abandoned him. She was a criminal and would likely be sent back to jail very soon. His best and only friends were trying to help her. And yet, watching Heather brush that tear from her face made him feel as though his problems were very small indeed.

Eighth Avenue
Early evening

"What if he doesn't show up?" asked Jake. "What if he's gone out for the night? What if he's hanging out with his girlfriend? What if he's gone on vacation?"

Since he had no answers to Jake's questions, Peter remained silent. His fingers drummed the steering wheel of his car. His father's large 35mm camera with a telephoto lens sat in his lap. A mosquito buzzed and skittered against the windshield. A car, half a block down the street, shook with the booming rhythm coming from its sound system.

He and the others had been sitting, crammed in Peter's Volkswagen, for a little over an hour. They were watching the traffic on Eighth Avenue from the relative safety of a convenience store parking lot at the top of the block. Generally the passing cars trudged down the long road like hikers in mud, pausing at the frequent traffic stops, inching ahead when the colors changed. Many of the drivers honked at cars that went too slowly, or at drivers who were apparently waiting for the lights to turn a more desirable shade of green. Even Peter, who actually enjoyed this sort of thing—the waiting, the watching—found his patience tested. His back ached. A muscle in his rear end cramped.

"I don't want to sound like I'm complaining, Peter," said Byte, "but I kind of agree with Jake. This guy might not show up at all."

"We know he lives on this block," said Peter. "He's got to come home sometime. If he doesn't show up tonight, we'll just come back tomorrow."

"So basically," said Jake, "you're saying this is where police work gets really exciting."

Robin leaned forward from the back seat, peering at the signs in the convenience store window: *Free cookie with purchase of large Coke! Popcorn Chicken—.79!* "If I thought there was anything better than a corn dog in that convenience store," she said, "I'd run in for something to eat." She continued gazing as though considering the idea. "Having said that," she added, "I'm not about to risk my life for four hundred calories and eighteen grams of fat."

"I'm fantasizing about a burrito," said Byte.

Robin agreed. "Yeah, maybe for a good burrito I'd take my chances."

"I'm not in the mood for Mexican," said Jake.

"Shush," said Peter.

A car half a block away pulled off the road and into a small parking lot next to an apartment building. A young man dressed in work jeans and white T-shirt stepped from it. Peter raised the camera and studied the man through its lens. Gray streaks slashed across the man's clothing—exactly the sort of look Peter would expect from someone who'd wiped wet concrete from his fingers after laying down brick for eight hours. He focused more tightly on the man's face.

"That's him."

"That's the guy?" asked Jake, reaching for his own camera. "Darn. For a minute I thought we were going to eat."

Peter was already stepping from the car, camera hanging from the strap across his shoulder. Jerome the bricklayer had pocketed his keys and was heading toward the apartment complex. As Peter hurried ahead, he heard the door slam on Jake's side of the car, followed by heavy footsteps on pavement.

A moment later Robin's voice called out from quite a ways behind him. "Guys!" she shouted. "Hey, guys!"

Peter turned. Neither Byte nor Robin had gotten out of the car. The boys hadn't remembered to move a seat-back forward so the girls could climb out.

"Oops," Jake said.

He took two steps in the direction of the car, but Robin stopped him with a roll of her eyes. "Too late!" she shouted. "Forget it!" Peter heard a loud *ooof*. After a few moments, the two girls stepped out. Peter winced when the car door slammed.

Robin and Byte caught up with him, leaving Jake to bring up the rear. "Don't say anything," said Robin, glaring. "Just don't say a word."

Jerome's apartment was on the second floor. The Misfits found him at the top of a rusty, wrought-iron staircase that dead-ended into a concrete walkway running along the length of the building. The scene reminded Peter of movies set in prisons. Identical doors stood every twenty feet or so, their faces sun damaged and their finishes webbed with cracks. Jerome's key was in the door, and he was jiggling the knob, working the key back and forth, jiggling the knob again. The door rattled as he gripped the knob and shook it, startling two feral cats in a dumpster below. They leaped out and dashed across the parking lot, shooting beneath a parked car.

Peter sprang up the steps just as the apartment door squealed open. "Jerome! Hey, Jerome!"

The man reared back a bit as he saw four teenagers clanging up the metal staircase toward him. He seemed to quickly sort through the faces, deciding one or two were familiar, before his body relaxed. "Peter, right?" he said.

"And Robin," said Robin. "And these two are Byte and Jake."

Jerome shook their hands, silent. He stood with his arms folded, leaning his shoulder against the door, waiting for an explanation. But Peter had to catch his breath and gather his thoughts. So much to explain: why the Misfits were here, what they intended to do, what they hoped to accomplish. Jake was fine; he could have run up another two flights without getting winded. Robin and Byte's breathing had begun to slow. But Peter was still leaning over, breath huffing, fingers gripping the handrail.

Jerome bent forward slightly so that he could look down at Peter's knees. Dangling from about that height was the camera and its odd lens, which swayed back and forth like a cannon taking aim.

"What the heck is all that?" Jerome asked.

Peter breathed deeply, smiling. "I'm so glad you asked."

His full name was Jerome Adderley, the Misfits learned, and he had been very close to Joseph Underwood. Once the Misfits had convinced him they were going to quietly, and safely, take a look at the man who had likely victimized old Joseph, Jerome had agreed to let them use his apartment. Indeed, since inviting them in, he had become a sort of demonic party host. He changed from his work clothes into a Green Bay

Packer's jersey and baggy jeans. He dashed through the apartment, snagging a dirty shirt from the back of a chair, an open pizza container from the sofa cushion. He put on a CD, then hurriedly switched it for another one he thought they'd like better. He poured peanuts into a cereal bowl and tore open a bag of spicy hot pretzels. When he handed each of the Misfits a soft drink, Robin set hers on a table.

"That's gonna make a ring," Jerome said.

"Sorry," said Robin. Jerome handed her a napkin. She set her drink on it, walked over to Peter, and nudged his shoulder. He was kneeling by the window, aiming the camera and telephoto lens. "When's my turn to watch?"

"You can take over in a little while," said Peter. He had been busy setting up the Misfits' observation post, a place where the four of them, in safety, could watch the street for as long as needed. It was little more than the window, the camera, and a sofa cushion to sit on. Byte and Jake had set up a similar post in the apartment's bedroom, which faced around the corner. Peter hoped they would have a chance to identify Briggs, to watch and get a sense of the man. Robin tugged the camera from Peter's hands, so he took a moment to look around Jerome's apartment. The light brown carpeting was the kind managers put down in inexpensive apartments because it hides stains well and is cheap to replace. The furniture appeared second-hand but nice. Jerome's high school graduation photo—all dazzling smile, huge eyes, and cocked mortarboard—sat on a walnut table, sharing space with a generic-brand television set. The one extravagance, Peter noted, was the sound system, a 300-watt monster that looked as though it could blow out the opposite wall of the apartment if Jerome ever had it in mind to crank it up all the way.

"Easy to see where your money goes, Jerome," said Robin. She had gotten bored with the camera already and had moved to the front of the stereo system. She fingered Jerome's lengthy shelf of CDs and DVDs. "Seven CD-changer. Digital theater surround-sound."

Jerome leaned against a wall, slurping a drink, kitchen towel hanging out of his back pocket. "I buy music," he said, "but most of my money goes right into the bank."

From the other room, Byte's fingers made a clackety sound against the keys. She had apparently connected her laptop to Jerome's phone line.

"Thanks for letting us use your apartment, Jerome," said Peter. "That group of guys you were with the other day didn't seem too happy to have us around."

Jerome laughed. "We just get very protective when it comes to this neighborhood," he said. "A lot of bad people have come in here. We want to make sure no more do."

"What are you saving for, Jerome?" Robin asked.

"I'm saving to *move*," he replied. "I want…I want to get away from this place. I hate it, and now with old Joseph…" He stopped, swallowing and shaking his head. "I can afford higher rent, but the actual moving is expensive. First and last month's up front. Security deposit. Renting a U-Haul." He shook his head. "Whew! I figure getting out of here's gonna take about three grand."

Peter crunched a pretzel. "That's a lot of bricks."

"That's a *whole* lot of bricks," said Jerome. "But I can't wait. I've got twenty-two hundred put away right now."

Peter went back to watching the street scene through the viewfinder of the camera. Locked onto the face of the camera was a two-and-a-half-foot-long cylindrical tube, black as a gun barrel and as wide around as Jake's upper arms. It was a 1500mm telephoto lens, which essentially turned the camera into a picture-taking telescope. Peter watched safely from Jerome's second-story window, while some shadowy subjects loitered in the street more than a block away. Jake was doing the same from his perch. Terrell Briggs, if the Misfits could identify him, would have no idea that someone was watching him—or recording his moves on film.

As the sun faded and the sky went from steel gray to black, Eighth Avenue filled with a life that was very different from the life that occupied it during the day. Peter remembered the shrieking children and the haggard elderly people who walked as though something heavy was slung across their shoulders. But both the children and old folks were locked behind the doors of their apartments now, the only evidence of their existence the blue, flickering lights their televisions threw against the windows. Outside, in the spill from the streetlamps, Peter saw figures moving. He couldn't make out faces, but the thin, muscular frames and lithe movements suggested these were young people. The shadowy figures moved in from alleys, from doorways, from around corners. Occasionally sudden, harsh laughter would come from the shadows, and Peter's muscles would jump inside his skin. One of the figures passed under the light of a streetlamp, and Peter glimpsed a red do-rag wrapped around a man's head. In the distance, framing the scene like a grotesque mechanical monster rearing up on its hind legs, was the Skeleton Building.

"I'm hoping this won't take long," he said.

"No hurry," said Robin. "I'm having *such* a good time. What do you think Jake and Byte are doing?"

"They're in the next room doing the same thing we're doing," Peter said, panning the camera toward a small group of young men gathering near the street corner.

"Or not."

"What do you mean?" Peter murmured, training his eyes on the men.

Robin muttered something under her breath. It sounded like, "If they're not making out."

Peter lowered the camera. Robin was looking away—*humming*. "Excuse me? Did you say 'making out'?"

"Hmm?" said Robin. From the other room came Byte's laughter.

The spell worked: At the sound of Byte's voice, a full color, digital surround-sound image flew into Peter's mind, clear and cold as an IMAX film of Mount Everest. He saw Byte's lips pressed against Jake's, her hand slipping off her computer mouse to touch his cheek. Peter agonized a moment or two, then mentally crushed the image. He brushed the hair from his eyes and threw a nasty look at Robin.

She stared at him. "What's the matter?"

"You put something in my head."

The mental image evaporated completely when a black Mustang came down the street, glinted momentarily in the light of the streetlamp, then pulled to a stop near the group of young men. One of them slipped to the driver's side window, and a few hushed words passed between him and the driver. The man's hand moved toward the window, then just as quickly moved away, dipping into his pocket. The move was quick, just an eye-blink slower than Mattie performing one of his sleight-of-hand tricks. The man stepped away from the car, patted the roof with his palm, and the Mustang roared away.

Peter leaned forward. "Did you see that?" he asked. "I could be wrong, but that looked like a drug deal." Peter had loaded the camera with 3200 speed film—a special film designed to work in the dimmest of light. With it, a sports photographer could shoot clear photos at a night football game. Peter had a slightly different use in mind. He twisted the barrel of the lens, and it grew a quarter inch longer.

"What are you doing?" asked Robin.

"Using the lens to move in a little closer," Peter said.

Byte's voice called from the other room. "Anything happening out there?"

"Not yet," shouted Jerome.

Peter stared through the camera's viewfinder and refocused the lens. The distant images appeared quite close. Some of the young men strayed a little too near the streetlamp, and Peter could see their faces clearly. He snapped a picture. A tall, round-shouldered man—who didn't seemed concerned at all about being directly under the light—was speaking to the others. When he gestured, a ring on his right hand caught the light and glittered. It must have been huge.

Peter handed the camera to Robin. "Check out that guy," he said, "and tell me what you think."

Robin twisted the lens ring back and forth, finding the clearest view. "I can tell you the jeans he's wearing go for about three hundred bucks a pair. And the jersey's another two hundred at least."

"How do you know?"

"Because I've seen them advertised in catalogs," said Robin. "They sell them in places I can't afford to shop." She snapped several pictures.

"My turn again," said Peter.

Robin handed him the camera. "Killjoy."

Peter saw one guy playfully shove another. The man got shoved back, less playfully, and landed on his behind amid a pile of clattering trash cans. Then the game ended. The young man on the ground launched himself at the one who had pushed him, clearly intending to do serious damage, but he never reached his target. A third man stepped between them, moving with an athlete's quickness and grace. He caught the guy, spun him around, and sent him careening back into the trash cans. The one who did the pushing fared no better. He received a long, arcing crescent kick to the side of the face; the impact sent him sprawling. Both men stayed on the ground a moment. Then slowly the two men first rose to their knees and then to their feet. They stood with heads bowed in front of the man who had knocked them down. He gripped the front of their shirts in his fists and thrust them together, like a principal dealing with a couple of angry high schoolers. He folded his arms and glared.

And made them shake hands.

"Are you getting this?" Robin asked.

"Every bit of it," said Peter, snapping off a few more shots.

Peter studied the man intently. He was taller, more muscular than either of the others, and clearly had martial arts training. "Hello," he murmured. He then handed the camera to Jerome. "Hey, Jerome, take a look here. Do you recognize that guy—the big one?"

Jerome took the camera from Peter and peered through the viewfinder. He aimed it around some, played with the focusing ring, and then froze. When he handed the camera back, he looked as though he had just witnessed a murder. "That's Terrell Briggs," he hissed. "You didn't tell me you were spying on *him*." He stepped away from the window and turned off a nearby lamp.

"Is that bad?" asked Peter.

"I sure don't want him thinking it's *me* doing it."

"Tell us about him," said Robin.

Jerome shook his head. "Huh uh," he said. "He's bad, he's mean, and I ain't saying any more." He was crouched on the floor as he spoke, keeping his head below the level of the window.

Peter stared again through the glass. Terrell Briggs stood alone in the street, caught in the full glare of the streetlamp, unafraid of the light. Without the aid of the telephoto lens, Peter saw the man as a distant, tiny figure, an ant larger than the other ants. Briggs, his back to Peter, studied the street, the buildings, the rundown businesses, as though he owned all of them. Then he turned so that he was facing Peter. His eyes seemed to focus on the very window where Peter stood. *He's too far away,* Peter told himself. *It just looks like he's staring at me. He could be looking at anything. Another window in the building, a sign or storefront nearby, an airplane flying low in the distance.* The moment held for several seconds. Briggs didn't move. Peter felt something cold and wet trailing down from his neck to the small of his back. "Yeah," he said. "I think we should leave. Now." He started dismantling the camera and packing it in the case.

Robin didn't ask any questions. "Byte! Jake!" she shouted. "We're outta here."

Byte called back from the other room. "This *second*? I have to shut down the computer."

Jake and Byte rushed in, Jake hurriedly stuffing his camera back into its case. Peter headed for the apartment door, firmly forbidding himself from studying Byte's mouth for signs of smeared lipstick. For that matter, when had she started wearing lipstick, anyway?

"What's up?" asked Jake.

"Huh?" Peter needed a second to separate his concern over Terrell Briggs from his concern over what Byte and Jake might have been doing in the next room. "Oh. Jerome's ready for us to go now." He indicated the window. "That guy out there is giving us the creeps. Let's just get out of here while everything's still friendly, okay?"

Robin nodded. "Jerome," she said, "we're leaving. Thanks for everything."

Jerome nodded. The wet soda can slipped from his fingers and spilled on the carpet. He didn't seem to notice. "Okay," he said. "Okay. I'll show you how to get out the back way."

In the dark, the handrail on the staircase outside Jerome's apartment had grown cold to the touch, Peter noted. The wrought-iron stair steps made a ringing sound as he and his friends moved down them. Peter looked far down the block, where he had seen the fight take place only moments ago. Without the telephoto lens he couldn't see much—just flittering bits of motion here and there against a black curtain. The figures had retreated from the pools of light cast down by the street lamps. Peter heard no conversation or laughter. In an alley a trash can lid fell over, rattling as it spun on its edge. A sound like paper rustling passed overhead as a bat careened away from the outer wall of the building.

"Okay, now I'm creeped out too," said Jake.

They turned up the street. The worst of Eighth Avenue was behind them. Ahead lay the convenience store, its bank of parking lot lights throwing down harsh white cones. Bathed in one of these cones, only a block and a half away, was Peter's Volkswagen.

Robin's fingers interlocked with Peter's, their two hands forming a single fist. "Not that I'm scared," she insisted. "I just like to hold hands."

"Then why is your palm sweaty?" asked Peter.

"I thought that was you."

Just ahead, Jake had his arm around Byte's shoulder and seemed to be drawing her along. The open expanse of the street lay alongside her right. Jake stood between her and the walls of the buildings, the patches of darkness, and the alleys that lay to the left. As they passed one alley, Peter heard footsteps echo from it—or thought he did. He paused a moment to listen, but the sound stopped when he did. *An echo? Maybe...* Then Peter saw movement. It might have been curtains blowing in an open window, or a sign hanging from one nail, shifting in the breeze. When he turned to look, he saw nothing.

He started walking faster.

Footsteps echoed crazily—Jake's and Byte's, Peter's and Robin's—in a beating rhythm that would have washed out those of any pursuer. As they dashed past the stop sign on the corner, Peter felt an extra blast of adrenalin. Across the sign someone had scrawled a symbol in Magic Marker. It appeared to be a circle intersecting a square, a crude copy of the sign of the

Misfits. His fingers tightened around Robin's hand. Their wrists pressed together, and he could feel a pulse between them. Robin's head turned in the direction of the sign, too, so Peter knew he hadn't imagined it.

"Faster," he whispered.

They sped up together. Their footsteps shifted in rhythm, from a steady drumbeat to a fast pounding. Byte spun around, then seemed almost to leap as Jake burst into a run too, yanking her along with him. As Peter ran, a set of footsteps clambered behind him, loud and distinct. *It's an echo,* he told himself, *just an echo.* He ran faster. Jake was almost at the car now, with Byte half a step behind. He ran so effortlessly, Peter thought—as did Byte, who rode her mountain bike several days a week. Robin played tennis with her dad. Even Mattie kept in shape for his magic tricks and escapes. Peter's throat was seared from breathing through his mouth. A muscle cramped in his abdomen, carving out a narrow pain like a knife wound. He shunned exercise. He was the Misfit who studied chess problems, picked up encyclopedia volumes for pleasure reading, and made up his own logic puzzles. If he were a zebra, he'd once decided, he'd be the one the lion was eyeing.

The four shot across the street and into the parking lot of the convenience store. Landing within one of the cones of light felt a little like breaking across a finish line. A police cruiser sat two spaces from Peter's Beetle. He could see the officer inside the store, pointing at a glass display then blowing his nose into a paper napkin. Jake stood next to the passenger door of Peter's car, waiting. Byte had found Jake's shirttail, squeezing it in her fist.

Peter spun around, breath exploding from him, and stared down the length of Eighth Avenue. He saw no one—just shadowy brick walls, clouds moving across the moon, the eerie geometry of the Skeleton Building. From somewhere in that distance a cackling sound pierced the air. It may have been a bird, or it may have been someone laughing.

chapter
six

the Misfits found police Lieutenant Marvin Decker not at his desk, but at the police firing range, located in the depths of a basement beneath the station. Officially, rules at the firing range forbade unarmed civilians from even entering, but Decker's partner, Sam, was at the desk when the Misfits arrived. He got them into the range with a curt "They're with me."

Without a word, the desk officer issued each of them a set of goggles and what looked like huge, padded earphones. Peter understood why. Even from the entrance, and even with these ear protectors *on*, he could hear the sound of four or five police officers blasting 9mm handguns. It was like a violent storm, Peter thought—the boom of thunder just outside your bedroom window, echoing again and again and again.

Sam led the Misfits past several firing lanes—deep narrow alleys at the end of which hung paper targets in the shape of men. The thick black lines forming head,

109

trunk, arms, and legs reminded Peter of the officers' purpose for being here, and it momentarily chilled him. They were training to kill.

Decker stood two lanes away, cradling his gun in both hands and squeezing off several rounds. Peter noted his stance, an odd, relaxed cross between a movie detective aiming at an armed burglar and a football fan firing his remote at a television. Decker popped in a new clip, eyed the distant target, and swung his weapon up in a clean, practiced arc, squeezing off four more rounds. The image, Peter thought, was striking in its grace.

"Hi, Lieutenant," called Byte. "Say, are you losing weight?"

Peter had noted that too: Decker's paunch hung over his belt, but not the way Peter remembered. Peter was as observant as people come, and he was certain this was the first time he had seen Decker's belt buckle. Decker wore a white dress shirt with the sleeves rolled up along thick, hairy forearms. His badge was on a leather carrier at his waist, and his scuffed shoes bore a fresh shine. His necktie, normally black or navy blue, was a rich burgundy color with sharp gray accents. The most telling change? Decker had shaved. Usually his face was shadowed with several days' growth of beard, but today it was as pink as a newborn's.

The detective turned and patted his belly. "Twelve pounds," he shouted over the noise. "Guess all those rabbit food lunches my wife feeds me are starting to work."

Sam waved off the comment. "That's not it. He's been getting here early and tackling the police gym. His wife just had a baby girl, and now Marv here thinks he's Mr. Macho.

"Hey, watch it," said Decker. "I'm armed." He touched a switch on the wall, and the target began to travel toward them on a narrow rail in the ceiling. When it reached him, Decker tore it off its clamp and showed it to Sam. Light shone through two holes in the paper head, and four more spotted the upper left-hand portion of the chest.

"That dude is *dead*," said Sam.

Decker slipped his weapon into the leather holster at his shoulder. "Still got the touch," he said. He then looked at the Misfits. "You wanted to see me, huh? Let's go up to my office where we can talk."

He led the Misfits back to the desk, where they dropped off the goggles and ear protectors, and then he took them to a concrete staircase that opened into the police department offices. At the end of a long hallway was Decker's own office, which he shared with Sam. Peter smiled. This room was a reflection of the old Decker—the one who was twelve pounds heavier and had a scruffy face. Decker's rumpled jacket hung from the wooden coat tree in the corner, a yellowish spot of mustard near the pocket. An untidy heap of reports lay in Decker's In box, the top file folder sporting a ring-shaped coffee stain. On the corner of the desk, standing out amid the mess like a brand new Mercedes in a junkyard, was a brass picture frame in the shape of a heart. A grinning—and possibly drooling—infant stared out from the frame.

Robin reached for the picture. "Lieutenant, she's beautiful! What's her name?"

"Good to see you again, Miss Sutter," said Decker. He was speaking to Robin but looking at Peter. Mattie's absence no doubt made him curious. "Kathryn Marie," he went on. "Seven pounds, four ounces."

"Don't get him started," said Sam.

Decker blushed, and it was interesting, Peter thought, to see the man's face redden with warmth and embarrassment instead of from the pressures and annoyances of his job.

Decker sat at his desk and gestured for the Misfits to make themselves comfortable. Byte and Robin found chairs, while Peter and Jake leaned against Sam's desk with arms folded. Peter then told Decker what had happened last night, describing in detail the men the Misfits had seen and, of course, the chase back to the car—if there *had* been a chase.

The lieutenant swiveled back and forth in his desk chair, eyeing the four teens. "Eighth Avenue's a rough part of town," he went on. "People there get killed for saying the wrong thing, having the wrong facial expression, or wearing the wrong color jacket." He paused. "Have I told you lately that you're idiots?"

"Sometime in the last month, I think," said Byte with a sigh.

"Good," said Decker. "Remember that every time you want to go to a place like Eighth Avenue. Just say to yourself, 'I am an idiot,' and then don't go. You're trying to help the Marcetti woman?"

Jake nodded. "You know her situation?"

"More than I care to," said Decker. "Her attorney—" He searched his memory for the name. "Cheryl Atterbury, isn't it? She's called me two or three times, mostly with questions about you."

"Lieutenant," asked Byte, "have you heard of a Terrell Briggs?"

Sam let out a whistle.

Decker raised an eyebrow. "Terrell Briggs," he said, "is the head of a gang that calls itself The Edge. You'd be smart to stay away from him. I could set up a whole separate filing cabinet in here just to cover his list of prior arrests. He always manages to slip away, though—half the time because a witness refuses to testify at the last moment."

"He had it in for Mr. Underwood," said Byte. "Is it possible he had something to do with the accident?"

"What you're really asking is," said Decker, "if it is possible it *wasn't* an accident?"

Byte nodded.

"Gang squad checked Briggs out," offered Decker. "If he had something to do with Mr. Underwood, they couldn't find any evidence of it. The Washington boy, since he ID'd the car, pretty much forced them to cross Briggs off the suspect list."

"What about forensic evidence?" asked Peter. "Any dents in Carla Marcetti's car? Fibers from Mr. Underwood's clothing stuck to the bumper? Spots of blood? DNA? Is there any evidence at all that her car was even *in* an accident, other than the fact that Micah Washington says so?"

Decker picked up a pencil, tapping its eraser against his desktop. "The lab hasn't found any yet," he told them. "Apparently Ms. Marcetti's car was pretty beat up before the accident. The DA is upset about the lack of hard evidence, but he figures the kid's ID is strong enough that he'll get a conviction without the forensics. Eyewitnesses can make mistakes, but when they do you generally don't get a car's make, model, and license number all matched up." Decker leaned forward. He spoke quietly, drawing the Misfits in. When all the bluster left Decker's tone, Peter knew the man wanted to make sure no one misunderstood him. "Look," the detective said, "I'm on your side, but I can't help you if you insist on being stupid. Terrell Briggs is the type of guy who'd think nothing of shooting a man just for looking at him the wrong way. Carla Marcetti's car was identified by a witness who has all his facts straight. And even better, other witnesses have confirmed the general description of the car." He paused, tapping the pencil once more, loudly, for good measure. "I know you'd like to help Ms. Marcetti, but I'm telling you this for your own good," said Decker. "For your own *safety*. This is an open-and-shut case. You'd better back off."

Heather Connelly and her mother lived in a boxy, ranch-style home on a street full of other boxy, ranch-style homes. Hers was the light gray one. Mattie's fists hunkered down deep into the pockets of his jean jacket as he stared at her front door. It was white, with tiny splits in the wood and scratches at the bottom where a cat had often marked its displeasure at being put outside.

Mattie pressed the doorbell. An infant began crying inside, and he heard what sounded like Heather's voice let out a loud groan of frustration. Then cooing sounds. The baby quieted. Footsteps padded across carpet. The door opened, and Heather slumped against the doorway. She puffed up her cheeks and blew air from between her lips, sending a strand of her hair flying as though it were caught in a breeze.

"Hi," she said.

"Hey," said Mattie.

She stepped aside so he could enter the living room. Its dull beige carpet was dotted here and there with spectacular color—children's blocks on the floor, a stuffed clown with a wide-mouthed leer, a tangled mobile, a springy baby seat on wheels.

"I know," said Heather. "It kinda looks like a bomb landed on Sesame Street."

In the center of the carpet, lying flat on his back on a blanket, was an infant boy. Mattie knew it was a boy because Heather had told him, but also because the baby wore a red pajama top and nothing else. He began wailing again.

"Sorry," said Heather. "He gets pretty cranky when his diaper needs changing." She knelt beside the baby and, with practiced ease, finished wiping and powdering him. In seconds she had him in a new diaper and excused herself to dispose of the soiled one. When she returned, she hoisted the nine month old to his feet and let him grip two of her fingers. He slowly waddled three or four steps across the carpet. "This," she said, "is Tyler. Say hi to Mattie, Tyler." She took one of his arms and waggled it at Mattie, saying "H'lo, Mattie!" in a high-pitched baby voice. Tyler grinned, enjoying the arm wave for whatever it meant to him. "Doesn't he have gorgeous blue eyes?" Heather asked.

Mattie overcame his urge to shrug—he still felt uncomfortable thinking about Heather as a mother—and instead smiled. "Yeah, he sure does."

Heather gathered the boy up and set him in the springy chair. "We'd better get to work," she said.

Mattie let out a breath—a not-very-hidden sigh of relief. Mrs. Molina's project on *Julius Caesar* was coming up far more quickly than Mattie liked, and he and Heather had barely worked on it. Mrs. Molina had given everyone some time to work on it in class, but twenty-seven students in one class meant a lot of distractions. Heather had asked Mattie to come over to finish it. Mattie looked at Tyler and figured the distractions here were about equal.

"Let me get my textbook," said Heather. She came back with her book and a bottle for Tyler. She moved the baby to the blanket and he soon fell asleep.

Heather and Mattie sat on the couch and worked for about an hour or so, reading through the Brutus/Portia scene and grumbling over the language until they had come up with a reasonable, modern translation. As they finished, Heather's face once again fell. Deep furrows grew between her eyebrows. Tyler wailed, and she squeezed her eyes shut as if it would keep out the sound.

"Did you hear from your boyfriend?" Mattie asked.

She lifted Tyler off the blanket, cradling him on the couch until he settled down again. "Yes," she said flatly. "He's moving in with his dad, who lives in Connecticut."

Mattie blinked, stunned. He felt a sudden welling of outrage inside him, like a fire starting in his chest and spreading. "Moving to *Connecticut*? Is he going to pay child support?"

"I'd have to sue him to get it," she said. "I...I was thinking I'd just hire a lawyer and make my boyfriend sign away...you know... all his parental rights before he leaves. That way he couldn't come back in fifteen years and say, 'Daddy's home!'" As she spoke, Tyler pressed his forehead into her cheek and gurgled a baby laugh. She kissed the top of his head. "But I don't have any money for a lawyer. And I just can't ask my mom for more help; she can barely make the rent. Oh, she's been pretty good so far, not complaining too much about all the extra hassles a baby brings, but it's as hard on her as it is on me."

"Hire a lawyer." "Parental rights." *How can someone,* Mattie wondered, *even a sixteen year old, take off and leave his own kid behind?* He hardened his fists and jammed them back into his pockets. He looked at Tyler, then at Heather, as he waited for the flush of anger to pass. He then found himself gazing around the tiny house, at the worn carpeting that bubbled up in places, at the pile of dirty dishes in the kitchen, at Heather's schoolwork, scattered across the table as though the wind had set it there.

"I can help," he said finally. "I don't know, maybe come over some afternoons and watch him so you can rest or study or something."

Heather stopped rocking the boy and looked at Mattie, smiling. "That's really sweet," she said, "but don't you think you're a little young to play house?"

"Aren't *you?*" snapped Mattie before he had time to think. He immediately realized it wasn't Heather at all he wanted to pose the question to.

Heather's smile faded. "Yes," she said. "I am too young. But I don't have a choice anymore."

They sat together on the couch, silent, staring ahead at a television set that wasn't even turned on. "My mom's in jail," Mattie blurted out. The words hung in the air like a slow-moving blimp. But Mattie couldn't stop there. He hadn't spoken to the others in days, and recent events were grinding up his insides. Heather was here, and she would listen. Mattie realized he would have shouted his pain at the stupid clown doll if she weren't. He told Heather the whole story: his mother, pregnant at fifteen, married at seventeen, divorced at twenty. He told her how his mother and father had left him to be raised by grandparents, how his parents had gone off to different corners of the country, putting an entire continent between them as though their hate for each other needed that much room.

"And your mom's in trouble now?" Heather asked.

Mattie nodded.

"And you're helping her, right? I mean, I've heard about you and your friends, how you do that kind of stuff…"

"No," said Mattie. "I'm not helping her. I hate her."

"Mattie, she's your mother!" Her voice shot up in pitch and volume. Tyler whimpered, and she held him closer.

"I know!" he shouted. Mattie caught himself and took a deep breath.

Heather fidgeted with Tyler's clothing, tugging at the pajama top to straighten it. She kissed his forehead again. "I don't know," she said quietly. Her eyes remained on her son, though she was talking to Mattie. "Do what you want; but I sure hope that when this little guy grows up, he's more forgiving toward my mistakes than you are toward hers."

Whatever you do, don't break the wand. That's what Gordon had said. He delivered the warning the same way Dustin's dad used to tell him not to throw the football in the house.

The wand was ten inches long and a little thicker than a flashlight. It rested in the back pocket of Dustin's baggy jeans, a pocket that actually ran from Dustin's behind all the way down to his knee. He could feel it bouncing against his leg as he walked across the mall parking lot. Malls were perfect for this sort of job. An ocean of cars to choose from, and most of them were expensive makes. Finding the right one was the only tricky part. Gordon wanted a 2000 model Mercedes 450SL convertible in silver, and he left it up to Dustin to locate one. Where or how Dustin found such a car, Gordon pretty much didn't care.

Just find one, he had said. And don't break the wand.

The mall was quiet today, which meant only scattered cars filled the outdoor parking lot. Dustin's Camaro was one of them. Most shoppers headed for the tri-level indoor garage that sat next to the mall itself. Dustin made a clicking sound with his tongue against his teeth as he pondered his problem: To find the car Gordon wanted, he'd have to scout the indoor lot, and he'd have to evade video cameras and mall security. *I can do it,* he told himself. *I can do it for Gordon.* Gordon paid him well. Gordon looked out for him. The indoor garage was dark, and the concrete walls and floor caused a sudden drop in temperature that made him shiver. Steel fixtures in the ceiling held fluorescent tubes that glowed bluish-white, and when his eyes adjusted, Dustin could clearly see row upon row of cars ahead of him. He began to walk along each row. He could eliminate most cars with one glance—huge SUVs or tiny compacts, cars the wrong color or cars that lacked a convertible top. Sometimes he'd spy a silver or a gray-blue sedan, but those, too, turned out to be something other than what he wanted. He moved to the second level. The wand slapped against his leg with every step, and he grimaced.

"Forget where you parked?" asked a voice.

Dustin spun around, jumping at the noise. It was a woman who was probably in her late twenties. In one arm she lugged a Sears bag, and the other arm was held captive by a four-year-old boy who gripped an empty frozen yogurt cup and whose face was smeared with chocolate.

"Yeah," said Dustin, "something like that."

The woman laughed in sympathy. "Happens to me all the time," she said as the boy hauled her away.

He found the car moments later. It sat with its top down, its white leather interior catching light like a snow mound. Dustin momentarily considered boosting the 200-watt Blaupunkt CD player in the dash—he had always wanted a system like that—but knew Gordon wouldn't approve. No one was to hear anything about *this* car—no news stories, no calls to the police. His heart pounding, Dustin fished the wand from his pocket and glanced around. He heard distant footsteps, some conversation, but no one seemed close enough to see him or note what he was doing. *Okay,* he thought. *It's time.* Dustin touched the wand's power switch, and a glasslike tube along one edge of the wand glowed like a red neon sign. The wand thrummed in his hand. Dustin knelt down behind the car and rested the red tube against the license plate. He touched another switch, slowly dragging the wand across the plate, and the device hummed even louder.

In four seconds he was finished. Dustin's breathing relaxed, and he stood, pushing the switch that would power-down the wand. The red tube blinked out, and he slipped the wand back into his pocket.

"Hey!" shouted a voice. "What do you think you're doing there?"

Dustin turned. Not thirty feet away was a dorky-looking white golf cart with the words Mall Security in black-decal letters on the side. Next to the cart stood a man who, in contrast, appeared not the least bit dorky. He was big, well-muscled, and wore a blue uniform with a security badge. At his belt was a nightstick, a can of what was likely mace or pepper spray, and a large walkie-talkie. Dustin had the nasty suspicion he was looking at something more dangerous than a typical rent-a-cop. This guy had to be regular police, moonlighting security at the mall for extra money.

Dustin ran.

His new shoes made a rubbery squeal against the concrete as he sprinted away. He raced between the rows of cars so the guard couldn't chase him in the golf cart, then ran toward the exit that would take him downstairs and outside. He ran with his heart beating in his throat, but he also ran with a smile spreading across his face.

His legs were strong and fast. His lungs drew in deep breaths of air to keep him going. The sun felt warm. Dustin ran toward the movie theater and disappeared into the exiting crowd. The guard wouldn't catch him. No one could catch him.

9:37 P.M.

Byte reached out her finger, held it poised over the keyboard… waited…waited…then touched the "enter" button. She hesitated not out of dread of what she might find but out of resignation, a feeling that as long as she had spent the last two hours messing around with this problem, she might as well spend ten minutes more. Her desktop computer, hooked to a DSL line, displayed in an eye-blink a web search resulting in over a thousand hits. Byte sighed and double-clicked on the first. Nothing. Then the second. Useless. Now the third. Boring.

The problem was that she wasn't quite sure what she was looking for, so narrowing and fine-tuning her search was a problem. She wasn't even sure she wanted to narrow it. She was fishing, and when you're fishing with no bait you can't be overly picky about the species of fish that come nibbling. Her current search—she swore it would be the last for the evening!—started with the keywords *hit and run, evidence,* and *strange.*

The fourth and fifth hit offered no help. She clicked on the sixth.

What really bothered her was that Peter seemed to be over his head in this case, which meant that the Misfits were all in very deep. He seemed distracted and uncertain—or maybe he was just responding to the one thought hanging in the back of all their minds: They were wasting their time. Carla Marcetti was guilty.

Seven. Eight. Nine. Ho-hum.

What's this?

The tenth hit appeared to be a page from a small daily newspaper called *The Ellesburg Crier*. Byte saw a photo of an elderly man, his hand touching the roof of his car as though he were petting a favorite dog. The car was a crumpled wreck, its front end bashed into the shape of a horseshoe, its windshield a blurry web of cracks. The headline over the photo proclaimed "Ghost Car Stymies Police." The article was short, only two columns. Byte shifted in her chair, crinkled her nose to set her granny glasses straight, and began to read.

When she finished a few moments later, she took off her glasses, laid them on the desk in front of her, and pressed her hand over her mouth. A little ball of nerves tingled in the center of her chest. The article made no sense. The *point* of the article was that it made no sense. And when a situation became so mysterious that no one understood it—not Byte, not the police, not the reporter writing about it— the best person she could talk to was Peter Braddock. Distracted or not, Peter needed to hear about this.

Byte bookmarked the page and reached for the telephone.

Peter sat up in bed, a legal pad in his lap and his favorite extra-thick, ergonomic gel-ink pen in his hand. He jiggled it back and forth as he thought, then drew a heavy black line down the center of the page, using a ruler to make it perfectly straight. He now had two columns. At the top of one he wrote the word "Byte," at the top of the other, "Robin."

Then he began to make his list.

Logic, Peter had decided, was the answer to his problem. Logic was always the answer. Even in matters as emotional as love, Peter was certain he could apply the rules of logic and learn something. With this sheet of paper, he would take love apart and examine its components. He would solve it as he would a simple arithmetic problem. Most people, Peter was certain, messed up their love lives because they let their hearts be their guides. He would not be so foolish. The heart lied, depending upon the person and the circumstance. The heart was easily confused by a perfume or a hairstyle, a laugh or a prom dress. And pheromones—well, they just turned the heart into a gibbering idiot. Not so for Peter. He would let his head guide him through love, and he would give his heart a good swift kick in the behind if it got in the way.

Here was the system he had devised: Peter would give each girl one point for a physical attribute and two for an emotional or intellectual attribute. The high scorer would obviously be the more desirable girlfriend. Under Byte's name he wrote the word "attractive." He hesitated for several seconds then wrote the same in Robin's column. *Hmmm.* He tapped the pen against the legal pad thoughtfully. They were attractive in different ways. He really needed a more precise word if he were going to score the two correctly. Perhaps one would come to him later. For now he just wrote a "1" after each name. Next, under Byte's name, he wrote "social conscience." Byte had often shown that she cared about the environment and women's issues, and those, he figured, were good qualities by any measure. He wrote a "2" after the notation. Now it was Robin's turn again. Under her name he wrote "extremely intelligent," though even as he wrote it he knew Byte was intelligent too. This made him wonder: Did intelligence deserve a higher point value because it came with the adverb "extremely"? Should he consider decimals? And sometimes Robin was so intelligent she was a real pain in the butt. Peter hadn't thought about *negative* scores. *Hmmm.* This plan wasn't working as well as he'd figured.

Brrrriiiiing.

The phone ringing, at this point, was a welcome interruption. Peter tossed the pad aside and reached for the cordless on his bedside table. "Hello?"

"Peter!" cried a voice. "It's Byte. You gotta see this. Get online. I just sent you an e-mail with a hyperlink."

Peter scrambled out of bed and quickly booted his computer. In a moment he was online, and a digital voice piped in. The voice was a download—Yoda from the *Star Wars* movies. It said "Mail you have, yes." He opened his mailbox and clicked on Byte's link.

"You sent me an article about a car accident?" Peter asked.

"No—read it!" Peter could almost hear Byte bouncing on the balls of her feet with excitement. "The car was used in a convenience store robbery. The robber wore a mask, but the clerk got the make, model, and license number of the getaway car. The owner of the car was arrested, but get this—he was a sixty-seven-year-old man with no criminal record."

"That *is* unusual," admitted Peter, though he still didn't understand why Byte was fussing so much.

"Peter," she shouted, "darn it, quit thinking and read the third paragraph!"

He read the third paragraph. He was halfway through it when he stopped, stepped away from his computer, and flopped back onto his bed. He needed to ponder this.

"I've got your attention now, don't I?" asked Byte.

The car had been wrecked, totaled in an accident that occurred two days *before* the convenience store robbery. When the clerk saw the car driving away from his store, the elderly man's car had actually been in a junkyard, pirated for usable parts. It was as if the car were a ghost, reassembling itself to take part in the robbery, then dashing back to the junkyard to fall apart again.

"How is this possible?" asked Peter.

"Don't know," said Byte, "but it's worth figuring out."

"Where's Ellesburg?"

"Illinois," said Byte. "Just outside of Chicago. I looked it up."

No help there. "Okay," said Peter. "Call the others. We need to work this out. If a car can be in two places at the same time, it might explain what happened to Carla Marcetti."

Byte said good-bye, and Peter hung up the phone. He reached for his legal pad again and stared down at the columns he had made. How many points did Byte earn for something like this? Should he have planned for extra credit?

Why wasn't this working?

chapter seven

Bugle Point County Jail
5:30 P.M.

here's what we know…" said Peter, in the cramped consultation room once again. Near the door stood Lt. Decker, who studied Carla Marcetti, the toothpick in his mouth twirling and shifting sides. Next to Decker stood the black female prison guard Peter had seen during their last visit. Byte and Robin, huddled over Byte's laptop, scanned the Internet for more information on Terrell Briggs. Jake leaned against the wall, whispering to Cheryl Atterbury. "The kid, Micah Washington, knows what he saw when Mr. Underwood was hit," Peter went on, "and a jury's going to believe him. That's the bad news. The good news is that we've learned about a…a *ghost* car—a vehicle involved in an armed robbery two days after it 'died.'"

Byte took over and explained what she had found. Her story caught Cheryl's attention. It must have been a hectic afternoon for the attorney. Her hair was wind-blown and one of her long red nails had broken off, making one finger on her left hand appear lopped off at the first knuckle.

"…And that's the whole weird story," Byte said. "No one can explain how the car could be at the robbery and wrecked in a junkyard at the same time."

"You're trying to tell me," she said, "that there were *two* cars, identical down to the license plate numbers?"

"That's exactly what we're saying," interjected Peter. "Which brings up an important question." He turned his attention to the woman at the table. "Who would try to frame you, Ms. Marcetti?"

Mattie's mother sat as before, clad in an orange jumpsuit, shackles clanking on her arms and legs. She stared at Peter through a veil of hair that fell across her downturned face. When the Misfits had entered moments ago, she had been smiling, and her blue eyes had seemed even brighter than they were the other day. But as soon as she'd seen that Mattie wasn't with them, her head and shoulders had drooped, letting her hair fall forward. Even now, though Peter had just addressed her directly, she didn't raise her head.

"Carla?" said Cheryl.

She raised her head slowly, first looking at her attorney, then finally turning to Peter.

"Ms. Marcetti," Peter repeated, "who would want to do this to you? Who would want to set you up?"

The woman sniffled. A little knot bobbed in her throat, and she finally sat up straight. "No one. I've never hurt anyone...." She stopped in midsentence, squeezing her eyes shut.

"Think hard," said Byte. "Isn't there someone who might want to get you in trouble?"

Carla still refused to look up. "Gordon," she said. "Gordon Moxley. We...dated...for a while. It ended badly." She shook her head. "But he wouldn't...it's not like him...he's in Chicago..." Her voice trailed off, as though she knew as soon as she spoke these thoughts that none of them mattered.

Peter tossed down three or four of the photos he and Robin had taken a few nights earlier. In one of them, a young man's finger glistened with a bright ring. Peter pointed to him. "Is this Gordon Moxley?"

Carla laughed. When she did, the weariness momentarily left her face, and she almost looked happy. The expression left as quickly as it came. "No," she said. "That's Dustin...Dustin Quaid. He's Gordon's flunky. He's just a kid—twenty-one, twenty-two maybe." She snorted. "Where did you get this?" Then she sucked in a breath, finally understanding. "Oh, my God. He's here, isn't he? And if Dustin's here, Gordon must be here too." She pushed the photograph aside and sat silent for a moment. Her knee began to quiver. "Oh, God. I knew Gordon hated me," she said, "but I didn't think he'd come two thousand miles to prove it."

"Why does this Gordon Moxley hate you?" Robin asked.

Carla's cheeks flushed a splotchy red. Mattie's cheeks

always reddened like that, Peter remembered, when he was ashamed or embarrassed.

"When I was arrested for my last...my last drug offense," Carla began. Her voice cracked. "Well, the police found a kilo of pot in the trunk of my car." As she spoke, her head turned in the direction of Byte, whose expression had turned stony and judgmental. "Look," she snapped, "I'm not proud of this, okay? I had made a complete mess of my life, and I was trying to fix it. I needed money. I wanted to get away, to move closer to my son. That was the important thing. Gordon could make those things happen, he said, but only if I agreed to deliver for him for a while. Gordon is a 'source.' He sells drugs to street pushers, guns to gangs, that sort of thing. I was in love with him—or at least I thought I was. I helped him for a few months." Carla ran a hand through her hair, a clumsy gesture for someone in chains. She sat up, and the Misfits could see her face, her eyes, clearly. "After a while I realized he was just using me as his mule. I was the one who was expendable if the narcs caught on."

"So you gave his name to the police," Jake said.

Carla raised her hands pleadingly. "I...I had to! Can't you see? It took me that long to figure out that I had to get away from him. It was the only way I could get my life straight."

"And the DA gave you immunity," said Peter. "You would testify against this Gordon Moxley guy, and in exchange you'd stay out of jail on the drug offense."

She nodded. "Only they blew their case against Gordon. Those *idiots!*" Her voice rang out, reverberating in the room. "The jury got to hear about my criminal record. They got to hear how the DA made a deal with me…and they let him off. Gordon walked over to me after the verdict and whispered in my ear. He said if he ever got his hands on me he would drag me to the top of the highest building he could find and throw me off. And…he takes pride in keeping his promises."

Robin was taking notes on a small legal pad. "So you came to Bugle Point to get away from this man?" she suggested.

Carla spun around. "I came to Bugle Point to see my *son,*" she spat.

Byte looked up from her computer at the outburst. As she spoke, Peter heard in her voice something quiet and…*razorlike.* "Ma'am," she said, "it's a little late for you to be pulling attitude about your 'son.' If you wanted people to assume you care about Mattie, you could have shown up here years ago." Her words settled like a frost on the room. Carla shrank in her chair; her fingers tightened into fists, and she buried her face against them, sobbing. Byte went back to her computer without so much as a blink.

Peter reached for one of the photos he and Robin had taken. He placed it in front of Carla. "Ms. Marcetti," he said, "this man's name is Terrell Briggs. Do you know him?"

Carla raised her head, tears in her eyes, and picked up the photo. She sniffled and shook her head.

Peter looked at the others. "Moxley had it in for Carla," he said, "and Briggs had it in for Mr. Underwood. It's no coincidence Moxley's flunky is hanging around with Briggs's gang. The two are connected." As he spoke, the guard took the photo from Carla, glanced at it, then handed it back to Peter.

"Hey!" said Jake. "Moxley could have 'encouraged' Briggs to steal Carla's car and use it against Mr. Underwood. It might be that simple."

"We have Briggs's prints on file," said Decker. "I can have the forensics team dust for them in Carla's car."

"That's a good idea," said Peter, "but there's something else… If Carla *is* being set up, whoever's doing it knows about us and knows we're trying to help her."

"How do you figure?" Jake asked.

"The other night," Peter said, "when we were running from Jerome's apartment, I saw—"

Robin completed Peter's sentence. "—a Misfits emblem drawn on a stop sign." Peter stared at her, and she smiled back sweetly, mouthing the word "sorry."

Peter ignored the apology and nodded. "It was a warning to us. 'Stay away.' The people in the neighborhood," he went on, "know we've been asking questions, but they don't know the name of our group, and they don't know our symbol. Someone—someone who knows us, who knows our emblem—has been feeding information to Briggs's gang."

He frowned, mulling over several ideas at once and rejecting each after an instant's thought. Who had betrayed them? Peter's attention shot toward the attorney,

Cheryl Atterbury. *Why? What reason would she have? Who else knows? Decker? Forget it! Rebecca?* Peter started to dismiss the idea, but the thought of the reporter lingered. *How did she get involved in this, anyway?* he wondered. *We never asked...*

A loud chirp from across the room interrupted Peter's train of thought. A frustrated growl came from Cheryl Atterbury's throat as she jammed her hand into her purse and yanked out a cell phone. She flipped down the mouthpiece and shouted into it. *"Yeah?"* Then, more calmly: "Yes, this is she." She listened a moment, rubbing her temple in little circular motions. "What? You can't do that!... All right.... I said *all right!"* She snapped the phone closed and tossed it back into her purse. Peter heard it clink when it struck something deep inside.

Cheryl turned slowly toward her client. "Carla," she said, "that was the district attorney. Joseph Underwood died half an hour ago. They're not charging you with hit and run anymore."

Carla shifted in her seat. Her shackles chimed. "What—what do you mean?"

"The man *died*, Carla. They're charging you with manslaughter."

An hour later, the Misfits were in the den at Peter's house, sprawled across the furniture like lounging cats. Jake sat back in a recliner, one leg slung across its leather arm. Peter lay on a couch with his hands folded behind his head. Robin, who sat on the floor next to Byte, took to playing with Byte's hair—braiding it, unbraiding it—as the group talked. A Tupperware container full of microwave popcorn sat on a coffee table. No one had touched it.

"Well, we've made progress," Byte offered. "We know Gordon Moxley wants revenge on Carla. And we know this Dustin Quaid guy is right here in Bugle Point. That's something."

"We know that no one actually saw Carla behind the wheel," added Peter. "And that her car was accessible, so someone else could have taken it." He shook his head. "I just wish she had a better alibi. 'I was home alone watching television' isn't going to help her."

Jake bobbed his head back and forth a little, as though weighing his desire to join in this game of positive thinking the others were playing. He finally surrendered. "We're pretty sure Moxley's here, too," he began, "but how he ties in with Underwood— He stopped, shrugging to indicate he couldn't come up with anything else.

"Wait," Robin said. "We know of two identical cars that somehow ended up with the same license number. What if another car, *exactly* like Carla's, hit Mr. Underwood?"

"But we need more than that," said Peter. "Imagine a jury weighing the probabilities." He raised his index finger, mimicking a pondering juror. "Let's see…(a) somehow another car—same color, same model, same license number—magically appeared, or (b) the lady's guilty. Now where would you fall on that one?"

"Peter," said Robin, "if it wasn't Carla's car that hit Mr.

Underwood, that means the one that killed him is still out there somewhere, right?"

"I guess so."

"Well, what if we can find it?"

Peter tapped his chin, thinking. "Finding the car would help," he agreed, "but the chances of that happening are practically nil. Whoever hit Joseph Underwood would have gotten rid of the vehicle long before Carla Marcetti was arrested."

"Okay, then," said Byte. "So the car's abandoned in the woods somewhere, or in another state. It's bound to turn up."

"It's probably been stripped and repainted by now," suggested Jake.

Peter reached for a handful of popcorn and shoveled it into his mouth. "No," he said, chewing. He felt a sliver of popcorn slip past his lips and tucked it back in, swallowing loudly. Robin was staring at him, so he dabbed his mouth with a napkin. "Byte said that the ghost car case happened in Ellesburg, Illinois, just outside of Chicago. Carla and Moxley both came from Chicago. Now, just for the sake of argument, let's assume Moxley was involved."

"Okay," said Jake.

"Criminals are creatures of habit," Peter went on. "They develop an MO—a *modus operandi*—"

"That's 'method of operation' for us ding-a-lings," said Robin.

Peter sighed. "Yeah. Criminals find one that works for

them and stick with it. I hear my dad talking about it all the time." He reached over and wrapped his fingers around Robin's hand, preventing her from starting another braid in Byte's hair. "Hang on. Byte, did that article on the robbery in Illinois say whether they ever found the car that was actually used in the robbery?"

"I can check," she answered. In a moment she had her computer up and the article on the screen. "Yup, it says here they found it. Same make, model, license plate, everything."

"Where?"

"At the bottom of a lake."

"Okay, then," said Peter. "Say Gordon Moxley was connected to the Illinois crime. He needs to get rid of a car, he puts it at the bottom of a lake. That's his MO, so that's where we look."

"What if his MO is that he never gets rid of a car in the same place twice?" Jake asked.

"Okay, genius," said Peter. "Have you got any better ideas about where to start?"

"Well, no."

"Then let's start with a lake."

"Hate to break it to you, Braddock," said Robin, "but this isn't exactly Minnesota." She indicated the window and, by extension, the bristling, desert-loving plants and trees outside. "We don't live in The Land of Ten Thousand Lakes."

Peter reached over to the table, picked up his mother's cell phone, and slipped it into the pocket of his jacket.

He grinned. "That just makes our job easier. Come on—
we'll need to stop off at Jake's first."

"*My* house?" Jake asked.

"You still own a wetsuit, right?"

"Yeah," said Jake. "But what—Oh *gawd!*"

Not sure what to do, Dustin just waited quietly while
Gordon finished smashing the telephone. It was a cordless model in a black plastic shell, and when Gordon
slammed it down against the countertop, the ringer
inside made sounds like a dying bird. A flying bit of plastic ricocheted off Dustin's forehead. He tried not to
flinch. Gordon snarled, then took what remained of the
phone and hurled it against the wall, where it clattered
loudly and fell, leaving a pile of wires and broken circuit
board on the kitchen floor. The bronze skin of Gordon's
face flushed to the color of an old penny.

Dustin had struggled to get used to his uncle's
tantrums. In their time together, he had learned only
that the best way to avoid being a target of that anger
was to stand still and say nothing. At least Gordon's
anger came and passed in moments, like a flash flood.
Dustin could see it vanishing now: Gordon twisted his
head so that his neck crackled. He tugged at the collar of
his shirt, brushed a bit of dust from the lap of his white
slacks. All the while, the redness was fading from his
face.

"I'm sorry you had to see that," he said. He made a fist
and brushed it playfully across Dustin's jaw, using the

same hand—now bandaged—he'd used to punch the stone wall in front of the restaurant. "Just some problems back home with the shipment. It's taken care of." Gordon moved quickly back to the stove and stirred the onions, peppers, peapods, and chicken slices that were sizzling in a wok. "Chicken stir-fry," said Gordon, "with just a hint of ginger. Too much and you ruin it."

Dustin used the moment to gaze around at the condo Gordon had rented for them, a two-story townhouse right on the Bugle Point Marina. It had five bedrooms— one for Gordon, one for Dustin, one for an office, and two extra simply because Gordon liked having more than he needed of anything. Gordon had also brought all his cooking utensils—boxes and boxes of them— which was good, Dustin decided, because it meant Gordon planned to stay here for a while.

Gordon spooned some of the stir-fried meal onto a bed of steamed rice. He then set the serving plate, which was piled high, on the table. With a wooden spoon he pointed to it. "Oriental stir-fry over steamed rice. You want some?" he asked.

"Uh, sure…sure, Gordon." Dustin remembered what had happened the one time he said no thanks.

Gordon whistled as he found two dinner plates and placed a huge pile of food on each. After arranging it carefully—"for presentation," he said—he tossed some green stuff onto the side of the plates and held them up for approval.

"What's with the twigs?" asked Dustin.

Gordon looked at him as though he'd asked what a

fork was for. "It's a sprig of parsley. For garnish—you know, decoration. Color. A little green next to the red bell peppers. Looks like Christmas, right?" He carried the plates to a glass-topped dining table and gestured to his nephew. "Sit."

Dustin did as he was told. He picked up a forkful of food and poked out his tongue to test it. Satisfied, he stuffed it into his mouth.

Gordon took a cloth napkin, flicked it so that it snapped as it opened, and laid it across his lap, chuckling. Then his face grew serious. "Dustin," he said. "You know I'm a businessman. I have some personal reasons to be in Bugle Point—you know, with Carla and everything—but basically I'm here to set up shop. I'd been talking about expanding the operation for a long time. Sure, I picked the location 'cause I learnt that Carla had run away here, and I wanted to take care of my business with her—but that's just gravy, you know? Frosting on the cake."

Dustin nodded, chewing.

"This thing with Carla is not good," he went on. "She knows how we do things. I thought I had her out of the way in jail, but I think we have to assume she knows we're here now. I understand she saw some pictures of you and Terrell out on Eighth Avenue."

Dustin stopped chewing and swallowed very slowly. A thick lump of chicken hurt as it went down.

"The problem is these kids," Gordon said. "The investigation was supposed to end with Carla. And if the police had been left to themselves, it would have."

Gordon used his fork to scoop up a neat mound of rice, which he then jammed into his mouth. He dabbed his lips with his napkin. "But these kids, Dustin, I'm telling you, they won't let it go. We sent a friendly message when they were snooping around Briggs's territory, but they're ignoring it. Now we have to show 'em we're serious. We're not playing around anymore." He set his fork down a little too hard. It clattered against the china plate, and Dustin cringed at the sound. "You know what I'm saying, Dustin?"

Dustin nodded again. Something in his left temple began to throb.

"Now, I don't like getting mean. It draws too much attention, and attention is bad for business. But enough is enough. I have two matters of concern. You know what they are?"

Dustin knew. Gordon was referring to the cars.

"Because you're my nephew," Gordon said, "and because it's time I showed you how I appreciate you, I want to give you something." He rose from the dining room and moved to a small lamp table in the living room, opening its narrow drawer. In the drawer, Dustin knew, were pens, pencils, a pad of paper, and a very large 9mm semiautomatic pistol. It was Gordon's favorite. Gordon moved plenty of guns, dozens in a week, but he had kept this one for himself because of its polished chrome finish and the (highly illegal) solid ivory grips. Dustin thought it was pretty funny when Gordon told him he could get more prison time for possessing the ivory than he could for selling the gun to a gang member.

Gordon returned to the dining table and handed it to Dustin. "Take this," he said. "I want someone watching both my...concerns. Understand? I don't trust no one but you. If these kids stay out of our way, we'll leave 'em be. Like I said, I don't want the attention. But follow 'em, Dustin. Get help from Terrell's boys. If the kids show up where they shouldn't be, take care of them. Make my meaning clear to Terrell. I want no problems with these kids. They need to know that Gordon Moxley keeps his word. I send a message; they should listen." With that he stabbed another bite of chicken.

Dustin's palm tingled where the gun touched it. He placed the gun on the table and rubbed his hand against the knee of his jeans. "What if the kids don't matter?" he asked. "What if Carla figures it out on her own?"

Gordon's cheek bulged with the food. He swallowed. "We don't have to worry about Carla." He reached into his shirt pocket and withdrew a handful of the photographs Dustin had taken at the prison. His finger tapped one—the short boy, caught sprinting through the parking lot and across the street. "Here's why," Gordon said. "This one is her kid. Carla won't dare talk this time. She knows what I'll do—not to her, to *him*."

The food in Dustin's stomach became hard and heavy. He remained silent and tried not to shiver.

"You got the wand?" Gordon asked.

"Mmph," Dustin said, grateful for the change in subject. He reached into the back pocket of his pants and pulled out the wand, handing it to Gordon. "At least Carla don't know about the wand," he offered. He hoped the reminder would be a little good news to Gordon, who seemed to need some. Gordon took the wand, and the news, without a word of acknowledgment.

He set the wand down and placed a hand on Dustin's shoulder. "Look," he said, "it's always been just you and me. We do it all ourselves; nobody out there in the world helps us, right?"

"Right," Dustin answered.

"I'm the coach; you're my starting quarterback, right? So I'm counting on you. I got no one else to count on. I need you to get to those kids. No mistakes, all right? I'm leaving this on your shoulders, Dustin. This is graduation day. You see 'em at the cars, you see 'em at the jail, you make sure they're dead dead dead. Y'unnerstand?"

Dustin bit his lip. This was a level of faith Gordon had never placed in him before—his boss usually took care of such matters personally—but Dustin could not let Gordon down now. Gordon had done too much for him. He was like a big brother. Dustin reached for the gun and slipped it into his pocket, though his hand still tingled at the feel of it. Nodding solemnly, he rose from the table and moved toward the door and the sandy beach outside.

"Where are you going?" Gordon asked. He jabbed his fork at Dustin's plate. "You haven't finished your dinner."

8:00 P.M.
Seabreeze

The sign was metal—tin, maybe—like a 1950s advertisement for Wonder Bread or Coca-Cola. It hung from a single rusty nail, suddenly creaking in the light breeze as though a ghost had leaned toward it and blown a spectral kiss. The letters on the sign, once cherry red, were now sunbleached to the color of rust.

Even in the glare of his headlights, Peter could barely read it: Seabreeze.

It wasn't cold, but Peter noted how Robin folded her arms. "This place gives me the creeps," she said. "And you're telling me people used to bring their kids here for fun?"

They'd had no troubling entering this place. The wooden arm that once blocked the entrance to Seabreeze was missing. Peter had glimpsed its broken hilt as he steered past it. Now he stood at a chain-link fence, running his hand along a length of cable that prevented the steel gate from opening.

"It is—or was—a man-made beach," he whispered. "My grandparents used to bring me here all the time." Standing between his headlights and the fence, his body cast a shadow that kept him from seeing what he was doing. "Here," he said, "hold the flashlight. We have to move fast. If a cop happens to come by, we'll be busted for trespassing."

He had been tugging at the cable as he spoke. If the car were here, someone would have had to cut this cable to get in. But where was the cut end? Disgusted, Peter gave the cable a sharp pull. The end of it snapped away from the fence, its broken tip nipping at the back of his hand. "Ow! That wasn't supposed to happen." When he held up the end of the cable, the sheared edge glistened like a new coin. The vinyl coating had been stripped off. "Just as I figured," he said. "Someone cut this recently. Then they wound the cable back around the fence here so it would look as though it was still in one piece."

"Peter," said Robin, "look."

A pair of headlights steered through the entrance and headed in Peter's direction: Jake's Escort. When it came within a few feet of Peter's VW, the headlights flicked off and the car coasted to a stop in the dim light. Byte leaped from the passenger seat. Jake exited more slowly with a large black bundle stuffed under his arm.

"Let's get this over with," he muttered.

Peter went back and shut off his own headlights. It was time.

The gate squealed as Peter opened it, its ancient hinges tortured by years of exposure to the salty air. Ten years ago, Seabreeze had been a family park, a place where parents could bring a three year old to play in the water. The sand and sea suggested the Pacific, but Seabreeze had no waves and, consequently, no rowdy surf riders. Eventually, though, its safety and tameness had come to mean *boring*. Teenagers, the most frequent beach-goers, rejected Seabreeze and spent their time at Newport,

Huntington, and Laguna. Also, an attendant used to lock the gates of Seabreeze at 9:00 P.M., so the place held little attraction even for adult partiers. It had closed after a few struggling years.

Peter, Robin, Jake, and Byte scooted through the gate and hid behind a concession stand with rotting timbers and a sagging roof. By flashlight they passed over the narrow beach, and Peter could hear a faint splashing and see light glinting off ripples in the water just ahead.

When they reached the edge of the water, Jake looked first in one direction then the other. "Aw, *geez…* "

"Why didn't you change into it at home?" Peter asked.

"Oh, that's smart," Jake snapped. "And I then get to explain to my parents why I'm walking out of the house after dark wearing a wetsuit?"

"Hmm. Good point," said Peter.

"I don't care," Jake muttered. He stripped off his clothes down to his underwear and began tugging on the rubber wetsuit, squeezing into it like someone trying to fill an empty toothpaste tube.

"If you think that's a pain," said Robin, "try panty-hose."

"It's time for everyone to shut up now," said Jake.

After several minutes of struggling, Jake was covered in black rubber from neck to ankles. A pair of flippers went on his feet, and an underwater mask equipped with a snorkel went over his face. When Robin handed him a large flashlight, Jake yanked the snorkel from his mouth.

"Hey," he said, "is this thing waterproof? I don't want to get electrocuted."

"It only uses three 'D' cell batteries," she replied. "How bad could the shock be?"

Jake started to pull off the mask, and Robin laughed. "Don't worry," she said. "Peter and I rented an underwater flashlight. The case is rubber, see? Break it, and you owe us fifty bucks."

Jake played with the on/off switch. "Are you sure this thing works?"

"Go on," Robin prodded. "You're safe, big guy."

Jake flashed it on and off a few more times to make sure. Apparently satisfied, he turned and headed into the water. "Hey," he said, "where do I start?"

Peter glanced around. Though the park was abandoned, a few scattered tire tracks circled around the sand in several places. He had no way of knowing if they came from a "ghost" car or from a few illegal, late-night partiers. He shrugged. "Wherever." Peter grabbed Robin's hand and pulled her out of Jake's way. Still holding hands, they watched as the black-clad figure waded into the lake. The flippers on Jake's feet made him walk like a duck, but Peter wouldn't mention that to him until tomorrow.

Byte touched Robin's elbow and drew her away from Peter. "I saw that," she whispered. "How's the romance going?"

"Fine," said Robin. "I mean, he's Peter, so expectations are low, but… fine. How 'bout you and Jake?"

Byte plopped down into the sand, dragging Robin

down next to her. "He's clueless," Byte said. "I could take a baseball bat, carve the words 'I Love You' onto it, and hit him over the head a dozen times. He still wouldn't get it."

"That's Jake," agreed Robin. "Maybe you just need to be more…direct. Peter didn't really get a clue until I had him in the lunchroom and was standing five inches from his nose. Maybe you just need to be, I don't know, a little bolder."

Byte covered her face with her hands a moment, not looking up until the feeling of warmth in her cheeks passed. "I'm not like you," she said. "I can't do that."

The two sat in silence for several minutes, following Jake's figure on the surface of the water.

"Did you see when he took his shirt off?" asked Robin.

Byte grinned. *"Ooooh* yeah."

At least the flashlight's working, Jake thought. He scoured the lake in an ever-widening fan, his face pressing deep into the water and the flashlight pointing at the bottom. In the beginning the water was shallow—far too shallow to hide a car—and Jake saw little except broken pieces of seashells and cloudy puffs of sand where he had kicked too hard. The amber light, glowing through the dark water, cast a green pall over everything he saw. Strands of seaweed stretched toward him as though reaching for his ankles.

He searched until his legs and arms ached, finding nothing.

Gasping, he finally thrust his head from the water and hollered back to the beach. "Hey!" he called. "Hey! How come I'm the one who gets to do this?"

The others were distant shadows on the sand. Very *dry* shadows. Jake heard Robin's voice calling back to him. "'Cause you're the one who looks hot in the suit."

He swam back and forth until the flashlight began to dim, its batteries fading so that the pale glow did little more than add a greenish tinge to the water. Still, Jake saw it—a lump, a hint of curved line, a flash when the light struck a mirror some twelve feet below him. After a few more moments, he turned, kicked his feet, and headed back to the shore.

He hauled himself onto the sand, feeling a little like a beached walrus. His legs throbbed from kicking. He felt lightheaded and dizzy. The water pressure had been a giant hand, squeezing his lungs. The snorkel had allowed him air, but not enough. Jake fell on his back in the sand, little golden lights popping in his eyes. He pulled the snorkel from his mouth, spraying salt water as he did, and yanked the mask from his face. He felt his chest heaving.

Peter grinned—not at Jake's pain, Jake knew, but because he'd already figured it out, which annoyed Jake to no end. Couldn't Peter just wait to be told like everyone else?

"Well?" Byte asked. She knelt at his head, leaning over him so that, from his perspective, her face floated upside down just above his nose. The effect made him even dizzier.

Jake held up a finger—*Just give me a moment to breathe here*—then nodded. "Better call Decker," he said. "Something's definitely down there. Just when I was about to give up I saw a glimmer of a mirror, a door…it's a car for sure. Looks like someone just drove it off the edge of the pier."

Robin turned to Peter. "Don't say it," she said.

"I knew it," said Peter.

Jake rolled onto his stomach and raised himself to his knees. From there he drew himself to his feet, his legs rubbery and a little numb beneath him. Byte moved in to help him lean on her shoulder. He felt her arm circle around his back; the other hand, the flat of her palm, rested against his chest. His eyes stared down at the hand. The feeling it gave him was both unexpected and surprisingly pleasant. He heard a rushing—vague, distant, like the sound a seashell makes when pressed against the ear. He shook his head, thinking the sound must be in his mind. But it was growing louder.

Jake raised his head and saw Peter looking over one shoulder at the parking lot. Byte said something Jake didn't really catch, but it sounded like, "This looks bad."

The roar came from a black sedan that tore through the gate the Misfits had left ajar. It shot around in a half circle, spewing torrents of sand from beneath its tires until its passenger side faced the Misfits.

"Everybody get down!" Robin shouted.

Jake felt Byte's hand shove against his back, sending him nose-first into the sand. He looked up in time to see a silvery glint at the car's windows. Two guns, bright in the moonlight. Fire spat from the guns' barrels, and the quiet air exploded, again and again. Sand puffed up in little explosions where the bullets landed. Jake felt a faint tickling at his scalp, something brushing against his hair. Behind him, Robin Sutter yelped like a puppy.

The car roared again, kicking up more sand and circling away. It shot through the gate, and the chain-link fence quivered as the sedan sped by. Jake watched it, the red taillights growing smaller and smaller.

"Everyone okay?" asked Byte.

"Fine," said Peter.

"I'm still here," said Jake. "Did anyone catch a face or a license number?"

Peter slowly stood, brushing sand from the front of his jeans. "No," he said. "But I don't need to see a face to know it was Terrell Briggs and his friends."

Robin drew herself to her knees and groaned. Her face and the front of her shirt were covered with sand. She spit some from her mouth.

"Are you all right?" Peter asked.

"Ohhh, fine," she said. "Just dandy. Everybody else okay?"

Nods all around. "My mother's cell phone's in the car," said Peter. "Let's call Decker."

He helped Robin to her feet, and she walked with him to his car. Jake tugged off the flippers and started to follow, but he realized Byte was lagging. He turned and saw her standing barefoot, holding her sandals by two fingers so that they dangled at her side. Her hair was windblown, and her dress was damp and speckled with sand. Her glasses rested uneasily at the tip of her nose. When she crinkled her nose to raise them, they slipped, and she had to grab them before they fell. A large moon glowed behind her.

"Is anything wrong?" Jake asked.

"No," she said. "You okay?"

"I'm fine," said Jake. "Fine."

She moved closer. Her eyes glanced beyond him, and Jake had the sense she was calculating the yardage between them and Peter and Robin. "Jake," she said, "we've been friends a long time, right?"

"Sure," he replied.

"Well, in that time," she continued, "have you ever…? I mean…" She paused, folding her arms in front of her. The silence seemed to last a really long time. She bit her lips as she thought, which kind of screwed up her face and made her mouth cockeyed.

"What…?" Jake asked.

"I'm thinking I wish I had a baseball bat," Byte replied. Jake stared. "Never mind," she said. "No, wait. Okay. I can do this." Her eyes locked on him again. "Jake, have you ever wondered if…?"

Another long pause.

Byte squeezed her eyes shut and shook her head. "I can't do this," she said. "I just can't." She threw up her arms in some sort of surrender, though Jake had no idea what she was surrendering for or to.

Jake shrugged. "Okay."

Just as he turned away, a hand settled itself on the side of his face, spinning him around again. A second hand joined it, so that he felt one on either cheek. Byte's face hovered inches from his. Then even those few inches disappeared as she kissed him. She pressed hard, so that his lips hurt a little and one of her teeth clicked against his. But it was a great kiss.

Then, just as quickly, it was over.

Byte pulled away, her glasses askew and her eyes wide as—well, the moon. Before Jake could say anything, and long before he could think about the possibility of a second kiss, she scooted around him and ran toward the cars. She *really* ran. The first explosion of sand from beneath her feet sprayed against his wet shins and stuck there. She slipped into his Escort, slammed her hand down on the locks, and sat in the passenger seat, staring forward.

By the time Jake got to his car, Peter stood at the passenger window, holding the cell phone and tapping a fingernail against the glass. "Hey!" he shouted. "We're not leaving yet. I just called Decker."

"Go away," Byte said.

Cha-chunk! Cha-chunk! Cha-chunk!

The beach lit up with carnival brightness. Decker had arrived, bringing with him three searchlights, a massive truck bearing a winch, and a team of two divers. They wore full tanks, with regulators that hissed as the men tested them. The divers wore sleek red wetsuits with rubber police badges embossed on the chest. The two carried with them thick chains that ended in steel hooks the size of a man's head. Peter watched as they strode into the water, following them in his imagination as they dove deeper, deeper, and slipped the hooks around the bumper of the submerged car. When they surfaced, they walked back onto the sand, pulled the gear from their mouths, and removed their masks. One of them signaled to the driver of the truck.

The lengths of chain lay slack in the sand, stretching into the water. Upon the signal, a great whining came from the winch, and the chains tightened. They rose from the sand, quivering with the effort of dragging the car out of the lake. Minutes later, Peter saw its roof emerge from the water. As the heavy chains pulled the car onto the beach, its hood gushed streams of water, and its front wheels cut tracks in the sand. The Misfits and Decker gathered in a semicircle as it rolled into view. The searchlights caught it, the dripping water glistening so that it hurt Peter's eyes to look at it.

But he had seen enough; it was a 1982 Chevy Malibu. Blue. License number 1XGP394. Its bumper and hood were marred with dents.

Decker stepped forward. "I don't believe it," he said. "It's Carla Marcetti's car."

"That's the beauty of it," Peter answered. "It isn't."

chapter eight

I *sure hope that when this little guy grows up he's more forgiving toward my mistakes than you are toward hers...*

Heather's words had been echoing in Mattie's head all afternoon. Now he lay on his back on the bed, his shoes untied but still on his feet, wrinkling the bedspread. His hands sat folded across his stomach. The ceiling here in the upstairs bedroom slanted sharply and was finished in narrow tongue-and-groove boards of knotty pine. Mattie knew exactly how many boards it took to cover the entire ceiling. He had counted them several times since returning home from Heather Connelly's house.

...than you are toward hers...

Pregnant at fifteen. Married at seventeen. Divorced at twenty. Running off, dumping a child in grandparents' care. In Mattie's mind, those facts had been the sum total of Carla Marcetti's biography. He had, of course, learned much more over the last few days. He thought of the sheets of paper describing Carla's criminal history, the way they fluttered from Cheryl Atterbury's fingers and landed, scattered in her briefcase like a conversation that never happened: Hi, son, let's catch up. And what have *you* been doing?

Mattie then thought of Heather Connelly—the way she was always cranky, the way her hair and clothes never quite looked right, as though she never had time to see to them properly, the way the skin beneath her eyes seemed puffy and a little blue. Actually, now that he thought of it, something about Heather reminded him of the photo of Carla that his grandma kept at the bottom of a drawer in her bedroom vanity.

The photo.

Mattie couldn't remember the last time he had looked at it, but the image came easily to his mind. Carla, just sixteen and holding a squalling Mattie, wore a yellow sundress and stood next to a swimming pool. Or was the dress red? Mattie couldn't remember. What he recalled vividly was her look—the messy hair, the flat smile, the hint of blue under her eyes.

Mattie sniffed loudly, consciously tossing the memory away. He had more immediate problems. His reaction at seeing Carla had made the front page of the features section of the *Courier*: "Abandoned Son Aches to Prove Mother's Innocence." He understood now why Rebecca Kaidanov, the reporter, hadn't warned him before she took him to see his mom. The shock made better copy. The article had appeared in the morning paper, and when Mattie arrived home, the pages lay open on the living room table. His own face was splashed across them. His grandmother wouldn't speak to him. He hadn't told her about seeing his mother. He had long ago stopped feeling. At first there had been shock, then anger, and then the numbness that called upon him to stay in bed and count pine slats.

Mattie sat up. Carla. His mother.

His mother, Carla.

More forgiving toward my mistakes... Rebecca had used his mother as much as she had used him. Maybe, he thought, he could look into this mystery—just a little bit. He didn't have to work with the others. He didn't have to speak to Carla. He could just...look around. A little. His feet slid from the bed and landed on the carpet. He started toward the door, but a shadow filled it before he got there. His grandmother stood in the frame, the pages of the newspaper wrung in her hands. Mattie moved toward her. He saw the flat expression on her face, the hardened lines around her eyes and mouth— and the urge he felt to circle his arms around her left him. He wouldn't be able to fix this one so easily.

"I'm sorry, Grandma," he said, "but I need to go downtown for a while. I'll take the bus, but can I bring your cell phone with me?"

She clasped him at arm's length, studying him. "Be home by nine," she said.

He nodded. His hand reached for the jacket that hung from the doorknob, and as he slipped it around his shoulders, he stepped past her.

"Mattie?" she called.

He turned.

"Tie your shoelaces."

The Bugle Point Courier
5:57 P.M.

A garden show. A freaking garden show.

Rebecca Kaidanov's fingers firecrackered off the keys of her computer, each stroke popping so that she could feel it in her knuckles and wrists. She was dutiful. She wrote about the time and dates of the garden show—twelve to five! She wrote about the varieties of flowers present—over a thousand! She wrote about new gardening implements—aerate your soil fast with the Sodbuster II! She had an ear-tickling quote from the show's director: "We want everyone to experience the joy and beauty of horticultural achievement."

She wanted to gag.

It was Mac's fault, of course. Mac was her editor, and with the exception of Rebecca's father, who had written for *Pravda*, he was the toughest old newsman Rebecca had ever known. Tough, that is, until three months ago, when Marjorie Kennings had purchased the *Courier*. Marjorie, in Rebecca's mind, was the Wicked Witch from Tabloidsville. Her company, Tattle-Tale Enterprises, owned three other papers, all of which featured front-page stories about Bigfoot, the world's fattest baby, or alien abductions. Now she owned one of the most respected newspapers on the West Coast.

Rebecca cut and pasted a paragraph so that it was nearer the top of her article. *Don't bury your lead,* she reminded herself. Her article now began, *Imagine a twenty megaton gas bomb with a scent like roses. Now you know what the interior of the Bugle Point Convention Center smelled like last weekend…*

A door creaked open, and she saw Mac leaving his office. He paused, slipping his loafers back on over a pair of argyle socks. Mac liked to knead his toes into the carpet as he worked. "Calling it a day," he said. "You still working on the garden show feature?"

Rebecca nodded. "Be done soon." Mac walked past her desk, and as he did the frustration Rebecca had been feeling all afternoon crashed down on her. She stopped typing. Her hand slapped her desktop, jiggling the coffee in her mug.

Mac sighed and turned. "You all right?"

"Mac," said Rebecca, "are you ever going to let me do real news again? I mean, how long am I grounded here in the 'E' section?"

Mac drew in a deep breath, and his shoulders slumped when he released it. "She'll get tired of this," he said. "Or someone will sue her for something she prints in *Tattle Tale,* and she'll get distracted by that. I can't see your 'punishment'"—he made little quotation marks with his fingers—"lasting long. I wish I could do more."

"And what's next for the *Courier?*" Rebecca asked. "Elvis sightings on the front page?"

Her editor turned away without answering, throwing his sport coat over his shoulders as though he didn't have the energy to slip his arms through the sleeves. His retreating image flashed in and out of her sight as he passed through the maze of office cubicles.

He'd been gone only a few minutes when something tapped Rebecca's shoulder. She yelped and spun her desk chair around. A short, skinny fifteen year old was staring at her.

"Mattie!"

"Hello, Rebecca." He sat on her desk and scooted over in front of her, then sat there, silent.

"Wow," she said. "I mean, you startled me. You're pretty good at sneaking up on people—not that I want you to ever do it again. How did you get in here without Mac or me seeing you?"

"I didn't *want* to be seen," said Mattie. He plucked a pen from her desk and slowly began disassembling it. It was the type with three different colors of ink, so the process took several seconds. Rebecca was grateful for the pause because it gave her heartbeat a chance to slow down. She watched Mattie for a moment, then reached into his hand and slipped the pieces of the pen back onto her desk.

"I know why you're here," she said quietly. "I'm sorry."

Mattie looked down. His voice was like icicles. "How could you do that?" he asked. "How could you not tell me my mother was going to be in that room? How could you write that article?"

She sighed. "Fair questions." She reached over the wall of the cubicle into another reporter's work area and grabbed a copy of today's paper from the desk. She slipped out the paper's E section and opened it to the article about Carla Marcetti. "Mattie," she said, "look at the article. Whose byline is on it?" Mattie didn't move at first. She folded the paper and set it on his lap, nudging his knee with her hand. "Go on," she said. "Who wrote it?"

He finally looked down at it. "It just says '*Courier* Staff Writer.'"

"That's right," said Rebecca. "After some new staff members got their hands on it, the story wasn't even mine anymore. I wouldn't let them put my name on it. The new publisher got angry with me for that, so now I'm back to writing—" here she punched the monitor button on her computer, and the article she had been finishing collapsed to a black screen. "—well, stuff no one wants to read. We're going through some…changes here at the paper, and you can't believe the pressure we're under. I'm feeling it. My editor is feeling it. That's an explanation, not an excuse, Mattie, but it *is* the truth."

"Are you saying you didn't write this?"

"No," said Rebecca, "I wrote it, but I didn't write it that way. I certainly didn't write that headline. Once the new boss heard your story, she insisted on turning it into trash, because she thinks trash sells. I wanted to tell your story *my* way, Mattie. Present the facts. Let the picture carry the emotion. I wanted to help you. I wanted to be a journalist who does good, the way my father taught

162 me." She tossed the pages aside and rubbed her eyes. They were dry and hurt, but rubbing them only made them burn more. "It's going to be a little while before this paper works like that again."

Mattie's face revealed nothing—no anger, no sympathy, no forgiveness. His lips seemed thinner, his jaw line harder than she remembered. He looked older. "How did you get involved anyway?" he asked. "How did you even know about my mother?"

"Her attorney, Cheryl, is an old acquaintance of mine," said Rebecca. "Mattie, your mom's been following you and your friends' adventures. She has clippings of newspaper articles about Misfits, Inc."

He let this sink in a moment. "And she had the attorney call you—"

Rebecca finished his thought. "—because my byline was on the clippings. Mattie, your mom insisted that I not tell you about her. She was afraid if I told you—"

Mattie interrupted. "I know. I know. She was afraid I wouldn't show up." He said nothing more, but Rebecca understood from his tone that his mother had been right. He wouldn't have gone to see her. He slid off the desktop and headed back toward the door of the *Courier* offices. Rebecca watched as he left. She had so much more she wanted to say—explanations and apologies, a story or two his mother had told her—so she called after him. "Mattie?"

He kept walking, only raising his hand to acknowledge that he heard her. "I have another appointment," he said.

7:03 P.M.

It was the worst taco Dustin had ever eaten—though he might have enjoyed it more if it weren't his fourth. Papa Bandito's was one of those fast food places where the taco meat was pasty and a fluorescent orange oil ran from it in dribbles. Now he felt as though a ball of lead sat in his stomach. He had thought this place would offer authentic Mexican food, or something close to it, but it turned out that Papa Bandito was a white-haired Scandinavian from North Dakota.

Dustin zipped his jacket up to his neck. The gun, tucked inside the shoulder holster Gordon had given him, jabbed him in the ribs.

I have two concerns, Gordon had said. He had meant the two cars—Carla's, and the one drowning in twelve feet of water at Seabreeze. As long as no one found the car in the lake or caused the police to get suspicious about the one in the impound lot, everything was fine. But if those kids came snooping around, they were dead dead dead. Boom. Graduation day. That's what Gordon wanted. For the past day and a half, both vehicles had been under watch. Terrell and his gang kept an eye on Seabreeze, while Dustin and one of Terrell's boys took turns watching the police impound lot from a window seat in Papa Bandito's.

Dustin smiled. He had an image of Gordon wrapping

an arm around his shoulder, patting his back, or even peeling off some hundred-dollar bills from the stash he kept in his calfskin wallet. "A little something for a job well done," Gordon would say. Then the image fell apart, like a jigsaw puzzle knocked off a table.

The truth was, Dustin liked the gun's ivory grips and the engraving on the barrel, but at the thought of actually using it, his stomach heaved. The *truth* was, these kids were only trying to help Carla, and Dustin… Well, he would never say it in front of Gordon, but he thought Carla was kind of okay. She had always treated him well, sneaking him a hamburger or peanut butter sandwich when Gordon was cooking something a little too highbrow for Dustin's tastes. Sure, she shouldn't have ratted Gordon out, but Dustin had a niggling feeling in the back of his mind that Gordon would have done the same thing if he had been in Carla's place—only he would have done it quicker.

The door to Papa Bandito's opened, and the guard from the impound lot swaggered in for his evening meal. He ordered without looking at the lighted sign that served as a menu. Dustin heard him warn the order-taker to make sure the cook put in extra cheese. A moment later, Dustin turned his head away when the guard walked past him carrying a greasy paper sack. He left, crossed the street, jabbed an accusing finger at a car in the intersection, then returned to the impound lot. Dustin could see him even now, standing in the little shack, eating.

Dustin hugged his jacket even more tightly around him. The shoulder holster chafed his armpit.

7:09 P.M.

The traffic signals, the occasional street lamp, and the neon sign over a video store gave enough light for Mattie to see his way to the police impound lot. Here, the BPPD kept cars they seized when an owner was believed to have committed a car-related felony. A steel sign wired to the chain-link fence warned Mattie against trespassing, and though Mattie knew he could probably get inside quite easily, he chose to obey the sign…for now. A young uniformed cop sat in a guard shack just inside the gate, sitting on a stool. The guard had turned on a small lamp, which threw a sharp cone of light onto an open magazine. Mattie walked over and gripped the fence, shaking it to get the officer's attention.

The officer looked up, set down a half-eaten taco, and moved slowly from the guard shack. His palm rested on the butt of his gun. "Help you?" he asked. Mattie loved that. *Help you?* As though he wasn't worth the effort of a complete sentence with both subject and verb.

"I'd like to get inside, please," said Mattie. He pointed toward the blue Malibu parked in the far corner. "I need to take a look inside that Chevy."

The man grunted. Mattie took the grunt to mean *fat chance.* "This is the police impound," the officer said. "Only cops come in here."

Mattie had considered this possibility. While on his way, he had thought of using the cell phone to call ahead to Decker and ask the detective to use his influence to get him past the gate. But he wasn't even sure the tiny guard shack even had a phone. No matter. Mattie could call right now. He held up his index finger, turned away from the guard, then pulled the cell phone from his jacket pocket and dialed Lieutenant Decker's office. Decker was out, but his partner Sam answered. Relieved that someone was there, Mattie muttered a few words to him, nodded at the response, then handed the phone to the guard. "He wants to talk to you."

The guard put the phone to his ear. "Hello?"

A burst of noise came from the phone—Sam's voice, clear and firm. The guard remained silent for a very long time, and the voice became a droning buzz. Only once did the guard say "but—" and when he did the buzz went sharper, crackling in the phone's speaker. Finally, the officer said "Yes, Lieutenant," and swallowed. He passed the phone back to Mattie. "He wants to speak to you again."

"Sam?" said Mattie.

"I got you in," said Sam. "Now just promise me you won't *mess things up*. If Decker chews out my butt for this, I'm feeding you to my rottweiler."

Mattie laughed. "Understood."

The guard reached for the keys at his belt and unlocked the gate, sliding it back to allow Mattie through. Mattie scrawled his signature on a sign-in sheet and started to walk past him, but then stopped at the entrance to the shack, holding out his palm. "The keys," Mattie said. No subject. No verb.

The guard turned to a series of steel hooks mounted to a wall inside the shack. He ran his finger across a row of keys, found the right set, checked the tag, then tossed them to Mattie.

"*Thank* you," said Mattie.

His mother's car was not what he expected. He had imagined it as the car of an unemployable drug user and thief—rundown, even dangerous because the owner had not cared for it. Instead the Chevy appeared in relatively good shape. Only a few older looking dents in the front. Not much help there. The interior, he found, was clean except for sticky spots of soda around the cup holder and a crunched-up McDonald's bag stashed behind the passenger seat. A wad of gum sat in the open ashtray.

I do that, Mattie thought, cracking his gum. *You're sitting in the passenger seat, your gum lost its flavor ten minutes ago, and you're getting that dry feeling in your mouth—where do you stick it?* He paused, weighing this. He had never considered the possibility that he might be carrying little pieces of his mother inside him.

Mattie put the thought aside and went to work. The door had a side pocket, where he found a vinyl-bound owner's manual and a copy of the car's registration. The address on the registration was an apartment complex just outside the downtown area of Bugle Point. It was an inexpensive area of town, but it was certainly respectable. Twenty minutes from the beach—and about the same distance from Mattie's school. A photo ID badge in the cup holder indicated that Carla worked as a nurse's aide at St. Vincent's Hospital. In the glove compartment were AAA maps of the county and of Bugle Point itself, a purse-sized package of Kleenex tissues, half a roll of breath mints, and a CD wallet containing four CDs: Led Zeppelin, Boston, Heart, and some spacey-looking thing by a group called Electric Light Orchestra. The last thing Mattie pulled out was a wrinkled sheet of yellow paper, which appeared to be a receipt from a local dry cleaners.

Nothing was on the dash. Nothing had fallen under the seats.

Mattie shifted, bumping his head on the visor, which had been left in the down position. When he flipped it up, he noticed a transparent decal about two inches square in the upper left corner of the windshield. An X-Press Lube logo appeared at the top, and below it, scrawled in black fine-point marker, were five numerals. *Don't forget,* said a tiny cartoon mechanic, *it's time for your next oil change!* Annoyed, Mattie flipped the visor back down.

Nothing nothing nothing. He wasn't sure what he expected to find, but the pure, unadulterated *normalcy* of this car was frustrating. How can you find clues in gum wads and an Electric Light Orchestra CD?

Backtrack then, he told himself. *Where did the accident take place?*

He reached again for the glove box, removing the map of Bugle Point and spreading it open across the passenger seat. He found Carla's apartment complex and workplace, seven blocks to the east, and then the location of the accident itself—which was several miles to the west and a few more to the south. *Now why would she be in that area?* he wondered. *There's nothing there she couldn't have found much closer to home...* Mattie shifted to see the map better, and—

Ouch!

His head struck the visor again. This time he slammed the visor up, punching it in place with his fist as though that would teach it a lesson. Once more he found himself staring at the smiling cartoon figure, Mr. X-Press Lube.

And five black numerals.

Mattie checked the odometer and studied the numerals on the sticker again, frowning. *That can't be right.*

He looked again at the city map. Then he popped the door handle to turn on the dome light.

Yes, the map proved it.

He tried to fold the map again but couldn't. His hands were shaking. Without thinking, he wrenched it into a vaguely rectangular shape and tossed it behind the passenger seat, where it fell next to the McDonald's bag. He took his gum from his mouth and stuck it in the ashtray. He had to talk to his mother—now, tonight. The county jail wouldn't allow him to visit at this hour, but that rule, Mattie figured, probably didn't apply to lawyers. To get in, he needed to find Cheryl Atterbury. *And oops,* he thought. *I'll need this...* He retrieved the map and scribbled down the mileage figure from the decal. He also wrote down the mileage off the odometer.

Soon he was rushing from the impound lot, tossing

the keys to the guard and shouting a "Thanks!" as he passed. Down the street was a donut shop with its lights on. A perfect spot to stop and make a phone call. He jogged toward it, through a patch of darkness between the well-lit impound lot and the next few buildings. He felt an oddly controlled giddiness, wanting to sprint but resisting the urge, wanting to believe what he had found but afraid to trust his mother. He *had* found something, though. Something that might help her. And he had found it himself, without the help of the others. It was a great night.

Mattie felt a hard yank on his right arm. His feet flew out from under him and he was propelled into an alley between buildings. The front of his body smacked against brick. Something hard and metal pressed behind his left ear. Mattie heard a *click,* then felt a vibration where the metal touched bone.

A voice said, "Keep your mouth shut. Turn around slowly and don't make a sound."

Mattie turned slowly, his hands away from his sides and his palms out. The metal object—a semiautomatic pistol—moved to press against his forehead. The gunman looked to be in his early twenties. Portions of his sweaty face glistened where little slivers of neon light from nearby stores struck it—blue at the tip of his nose, red above one eyebrow, a yellow slice across the chin. On his hand was a huge ring that spread over two fingers, spelling L-O-V-E in glittery letters. Mostly, though, Mattie just saw the gun. It seemed shake a little, as though the man was unaccustomed to holding it.

"What were you doing, messing around with that car?"
"It belongs to my mother," said Mattie.

The man's eyebrows crinkled. He bit his lip, and he seemed to be calculating what to do next. The gun hand lowered some, but when Mattie shifted his weight, dragging a foot across the asphalt, the gun flew back up.

"Don't move!"

"I'm not moving," Mattie reassured him.

The man glanced over his shoulder, swallowing thickly. "You're—you're Ramiro, then? Carla's kid?"

Mattie nodded. *Carla. Whoever this guy is, he's on a first name basis with my mother.*

The man looked away from Mattie's face, muttering to himself. "What do I do? What do I do?" he asked. He reminded Mattie of a child who had gotten lost in a crowded mall. He made nodding motions with his head, carrying on a silent conversation with himself. "Okay," he said finally, "okay then. I'm not gonna kill you."

Mattie wasn't sure what to say. What came out was, "Thanks."

The man backed away into the darkness. "But stay away from this car. If I catch you around here again, I *will* hurt you." As if to punctuate the idea, he pointed the barrel of the gun straight up and clicked the hammer back into place. Mattie felt a sympathetic tingle behind his ear.

The man was gone. Mattie heard footsteps running, then a shimmering sound as the man hit a chain-link fence and hauled himself over. Mattie slumped against the wall. He sat down on the pavement. *Breathe,* he told himself. His calf muscles tingled, as though both of his legs had fallen asleep and were now waking up.

The man had pointed a gun at him. The man knew his name, knew his mother's name. Indeed, the fact that Mattie was Carla's son had stopped the man from shooting him.

Mattie slipped into the donut shop, collapsed at a table, and reached into his jacket pocket for the cell phone. He let Directory Assistance find the number for attorney Cheryl Atterbury. A sharp voice answered on the first ring.

"Hello?"

"Ms. Atterbury?" said Mattie. "I need to talk to you. You and…Carla."

A pause. "Who is this?"

Mattie sat up a little straighter. "I'm Mattie Ramiro," he said. "Carla Marcetti's son."

Cheryl Atterbury stood in the corner of the conference room, arms folded. She wore a summer dress, pale blue and cut off well above the knees. Mattie's call had no doubt interrupted preparations for a date. Mattie heard a rattling of keys and turned to the gray door at the rear of the room.

The door opened, and a tall male guard led Carla in. She sat at the table, silent. Her eyes flickered toward her lawyer for only an instant before settling on Mattie. She stared as though trying to take in everything about him. As for Mattie, he did much the same, noting for the first time that the darkness that once lined the underside of his mother's eyes now completely encircled them. Her hair was longish and straight, and in a gesture Mattie thought he recalled, she reached up and combed her fingers through it. Only now, of course, she had to use both hands, since they were chained together at the wrists. She had been chewing her nails, he noted, but only on the right hand. Her knee bounced up and down nervously as he watched her.

"So what's this about?" asked the attorney.

Mattie pulled from his jacket the map of Bugle Point he'd taken from the Chevy and opened it out on the table. Cheryl Atterbury cocked an eyebrow and walked over to join him.

"The day before the accident with Mr. Underwood," Mattie began, "Umm…Carla…took her car in for an oil change." His index finger landed on the number he had written. "The mechanic put a decal in the windshield showing the mileage when her next oil change was due."

"In three thousand miles," said the attorney.

"Right," said Mattie, "so if we subtract three thousand from the number on the decal, we know exactly what the mileage was on her car when she took it to the mechanic."

"Sure," said the attorney. "The mechanic looks at the mileage on the odometer, adds three thousand miles to it, and writes that number on the decal."

Carla leaned forward, listening.

Mattie unfolded the map and pointed at the second number he had written. "This," he said, "is the odometer reading on the car right now. See the difference?"

"It's seventeen miles more than it was at the mechanic's shop," said Cheryl.

Mattie smiled. "Exactly." He turned now to the map, where he had drawn two small circles. He pointed them out to the attorney. "Here's the location of the lube shop," he said, "and here's the corner where Mr. Underwood was hit by a Chevy Malibu, fourteen miles away."

The woman frowned. "So?" She didn't get it—which, for some reason, added to Mattie's delight.

"Well," he said, "Carla supposedly drove her Malibu from the accident site back to her apartment, twelve miles away. That's where the police arrested her, remember? Adding another twelve miles makes *twenty-six*, not seventeen."

Dawn finally rose in Cheryl Atterbury's face. "But that's impossible."

Mattie leaned back in his chair. "Right. Carla was nowhere near Eighth Avenue when Joseph Underwood was hit. She couldn't have been, because her car hadn't been driven that far."

"Is…is that it, then?" asked Carla. "Does that prove I'm innocent?"

Carla and Cheryl Atterbury exchanged glances. The attorney then reached down and plucked the map from the table. "May I?" she asked. "I'll need this to file a motion to dismiss the charges."

"You can get the charges dropped?" Mattie asked.

She shook her head. "Probably not. The DA will say that the mechanic made a mistake when he wrote the mileage down, or that someone rolled back the odometer. The judge will say it's a question of fact, something for a jury to decide." She folded the items into a beaded purse. "What this gives us, Carla, is a strong case for reasonable doubt. We're still going to trial, but we have a much better chance of winning." She paused before delivering an afterthought: "I *think.*"

Mattie looked at the attorney and for the first time noticed how young she really was. In the right clothes, Cheryl Atterbury might pass for an upperclassman at the high school. The thought made a line of cold crawl up Mattie's back. Just how much did this woman know about law?

"Excuse me," he asked. "No offense—but how many cases have you won?"

The woman stiffened. A full five seconds passed before she answered. "Well…three."

"*Three?*"

The attorney's hand flipped over and then flipped back, like a tiny version of a shrug. To Mattie, the gesture looked like an apology. "Well—three in moot court."

The word "moot" somehow fed Mattie's sense of horror. "What's moot court?" he asked.

"Um…it's where law students practice trying cases before they go in front of a real court."

Mattie's head fell into his hands. He closed his eyes. "You've never won a case."

"Well, that's not exactly fair," he heard her say. "I've never lost one either. Carla's my first."

"You've *never* tried a case?" Mattie cried.

"Hey," snapped the attorney, "back off! I just passed the bar exam three months ago, and I'm working here as a public defender. It was the luck of the draw, and Carla got me."

Mattie nodded and rose from the table. The attorney would do the best she could. He pushed his chair back in and knocked on the door for the guard.

"Mattie?" said a voice.

It was almost a whisper, and it had not come from the attorney. Mattie, his hand already on the doorknob, turned and looked at his mother. He realized then she had hardly spoken the entire time he had been here. For a moment he wondered why, then he remembered that the last two times she had spoken to him, he had run from the room. Her knee had stopped bouncing some minutes ago, but now it started again.

"You do believe me now?" she asked. "That maybe I'm not such a bad person?"

Mattie stared at his mother. "I—I don't know," he said. Then he left, hearing the lock click like a shot behind him.

chapter nine

the fluorescent lights in the ceiling of Decker's office filled the room with a cold whiteness. Peter squinted until his eyes adjusted. Less than an hour ago he had stood on the sands of the abandoned beach called Seabreeze, and his eyes still remembered the pale glow of his headlights and the yellow searchlights pointed at the water. Jake sat across the room, on a corner of Sam's desktop. Byte and Robin sat in a pair of chrome chairs facing the Lieutenant. Decker leaned back at his desk, the chair creaking underneath him. "Okay, first of all," he said, twirling a pen in his fingers, "before you went snooping around in an area full of gangs, drugs, and guns, and before you decided to break into private property and go snorkeling in the dark—what should you have done?" He paused, waiting for an answer.

Byte crinkled her nose to set her glasses straight. "Say 'I am an idiot'?

Decker exploded. "You *are* idiots! What were you thinking? You've worked on only a handful of cases, and this is the second time you've been in a situation where someone has taken shots at you."

"Third time, I think," said Jake. "There was the guy at the comic convention who…"

Decker shot him a look, and Jake stopped in mid-sentence. "Okay, then," Decker said. " Now tell me about the shooting."

"It was a black sedan of some kind," said Peter. "Four doors—or at least that's what I figure, since it seemed that guns were sticking out of two sets of windows."

Decker looked at the others, waiting to hear more. Jake shook his head. Robin and Byte shared a glance, as though each was expecting the other to offer something. Neither did.

"It was dark, Lieutenant," said Robin. "And we kinda had our faces in the sand."

"It was Terrell Briggs and his gang," said Peter. "I know it. He tried to scare us away from Eighth Avenue, and tonight he tried to keep us from finding the car."

"You don't have proof, though," said the Lieutenant. He stared up at the ceiling, rocking his desk chair back and forth as he thought. "Terrell Briggs has been a problem for our gang unit for a couple of years now. He's surprisingly smart for someone whose only goal is to own a stretch of Eighth Avenue. We've never been able to get enough on him to make a charge stick."

"He may be more ambitious now," said Peter. "If it *was* Terrell Briggs in that car tonight, it means he's somehow tied to Mattie's mother—and there's only one person who connects them."

"Carla's old boyfriend, Gordon Moxley," said Robin.

"Exactly," said Peter. "I think, Lieutenant, you may have to consider the possibility that Terrell Briggs has some new plans. Carla told us that Gordon Moxley sells drugs and guns to gangs. If Moxley is in Bugle Point and Terrell Briggs is talking to him, it may mean that Briggs is trying to expand his territory. He's looking to buy drugs or guns to do it."

"Or both," said Decker.

Peter nodded. "Or both."

"Lieutenant," said Byte, "what about Mattie's mom? Now that we've found another car that's exactly like hers, even down to the license plate number, doesn't that mean she's off the hook?"

Decker tossed the pen to his desk and leaned forward, his elbows planted on the desktop. He laced his fingers together and looked at Byte. "I'm not a lawyer," he said, "but my guess is no. The fact that another car looks just like hers doesn't mean she didn't hit Mr. Underwood."

"It will, however, help to create reasonable doubt in the mind of a jury," said Robin. "Cheryl Atterbury can now show that Carla might not have been the one who killed Joseph Underwood. If we can just find some evidence that shows she *probably* wasn't the one, we might be able to get the case against her thrown out."

As Robin spoke, a faint rapping came from the doorway. A voice said, "I might be able to help you there."

"Mattie!" squealed Byte.

He had spoken quietly, and his shoulders were hunched as though he were a little ashamed of being there. Maybe, Peter thought, he just wasn't sure what his friends were feeling after he had gone off on his own. Byte and Robin gave Mattie no chance to ponder such questions. They ran over to him and dragged him down into a chair between them.

"Hey there," said Robin. "We've been worried about you."

"Hey, Robin," said Mattie, "Long time no…*urrrgh*…"

Byte had wrapped her arms around his neck and drawn him into a tight hug. "Yeah, we're glad you're back. We were afraid you were mad at us."

"Okay, okay," said Mattie, laughing. "Don't choke me." Byte released him. "So," he said to the group, "Sam told me you guys found a car just like Carla Marcetti's. I found proof Carla was never on Eighth Avenue. Let's get caught up on what we know."

"You go first," said Jake.

"Well, Carla wasn't on Eighth Avenue when the accident happened," Mattie explained. "I found an oil change decal in her car, dated the day before the hit and run. She *couldn't* have gone to Eighth Avenue and back to her apartment. The mileage showed she hadn't driven her car far enough."

Jake picked up the other half of the story. "We found a car identical to Carla's sunk in a lake. Same make, model, license plate, everything."

"So… it's for sure?" Mattie asked. "She really didn't do it? I mean, this has got to prove that she's innocent."

"Not quite," Peter said. "By themselves, neither one of

these facts will get your mom off, but maybe the two of them together…"

"This is all great," said Robin, "but I want to know what we do after that. Whoever did this is still out there. Carla's in danger. *We're* in danger."

The weight of that possibility hung over all of them. "And if Carla walks out of jail," Byte said, "it's only going to get worse." She turned to the lieutenant. "We can't do anything about this Gordon Moxley guy, because we're not even positive he's here, so what's the next step? Can you arrest Terrell Briggs?"

Decker shook his head. "Not enough evidence for an arrest," he said, "but if we can get any little tidbit of evidence, just enough to justify going before a judge, we might be able to get a search warrant. Then we could search Briggs's car, look for guns in his apartment." The detective paused. "And I know how we might get that evidence." He reached for a knob just above one of his desk drawers and slid out a flat piece of wood—a writing surface. On top of it was a sheet of paper, laminated and taped down. It appeared to be a list of names and phone numbers. Decker grabbed his phone and punched at the keypad.

"Hello," he said, "Mrs. Weese? Marvin Decker. May I speak to Marco, please?"

Robin leaned toward Mattie, whispering. "Who's Marco Weese?"

"Forensic scientist," Mattie replied. "He examines evidence in the police lab."

Jake, overhearing, slipped over and sat down with them. "What do you think he's looking for?" he asked.

"Marco," said the Lieutenant, "it's Decker. Listen, earlier this evening a car crashed through the gate at the old Seabreeze park. Shots were fired. I need you to go out there and see what you can find." Decker sighed and drummed a pen against his desktop, waiting for Weese's initial reaction to pass. "I know it's late," he said, "but you've done the impossible before. I need to hear about anything you find as soon as…. What? I don't know—a ballistics check on the bullets, if you can find them. Well then, *anything*…you're the scientist, for crying out loud." Decker circled his hand in a hurry-up gesture. "No, Marco," he said. Peter could imagine Decker talking to his new daughter in the same patient tone. "I'm sure it's fascinating. No…well, I don't get the Discovery Channel so I wouldn't know…. I'm sure it is. Then *tape* it…. All right. I appreciate it." Decker hung up. "We'll know more tomorrow," he said.

Mattie stood. "I could use a ride home."

"I can take you," Jake offered.

"Well, that'd be great. Buses have stopped running. Plus my grandma told me to be home by nine. I called her to say I'd be late, but not *this* late. I'll probably get grounded for a month."

"That's a bummer," said Jake.

Mattie looked at Jake's damp clothes and straggly hair, then at Robin's stained shirt, peppered with flecks of sand. The youngest Misfit stood silent a moment, his face—normally round, pale, babylike—knitting itself into something wiser.

"No, actually," he said, "I think it might be a pretty good thing."

La Femme de Désir

Dustin Quaid glanced in the restroom mirror at his new double-breasted suit with its pearly buttons, its faint pinstripes, and its tuft of handkerchief blooming from the pocket. The coat felt overly large, billowing out as he walked, and the collar of his shirt hung loose around his thin neck. He had tied his necktie three times and still the narrow end hung lower than the wide end, which had to be wrong. The pants were pleated and baggy, though not as full as his saggy jeans.

Dustin didn't have to use the restroom. He had left the table because his hand had started shaking and caused him to drop his fork. It had clattered against the edge of his plate, spraying little brown droplets of steak juice against the white tablecloth. He had covered the stain with his napkin, then excused himself and rushed to the men's room to splash a little water on his face. Dustin reached into the inner breast pocket of his coat—oh, how he wanted a long calfskin wallet like Gordon's to put in there!—and took out a package of chewing gum. He folded a stick into his mouth, doubling it over and biting down. The taste was sweet, fruity. He found it oddly comforting. Dustin, whose hand was still shaking, had learned something tonight: He could deal with wearing the suit, as stiff as it made him feel. He could face a cop eyeing him from across the street and talking into a radio. He could even face Gordon, if Gordon's mood wasn't too explosive.

But he could not face Terrell Briggs.

Briggs had sat at the table tonight, saying and moving little, like a lion listening for prey rustling in the brush. It was a mystery to Dustin how Gordon learned so much about their potential business partners. He already had a dossier on Briggs. Terrell Briggs had once gotten a scholarship to play football for Texas A&M, but that he had lost that scholarship when, as a high school senior, he had tried to sell several ounces of a drug—Gordon hadn't said what—to an undercover police officer. He had been only seventeen at the time. He served a one-year prison term in a juvenile facility, and his record was sealed because he was a minor. He then joined the military upon his release, trained briefly as a Navy SEAL, and was thrown out after six months with a dishonorable discharge. After a fight with another SEAL, he had landed in the hospital with fractured facial bones. Terrell still carried the memory of that fight in his face; his left cheekbone was larger than the right and knotted like a tree branch.

The bottom line was, Terrell Briggs scared the baggy, pleated, pinstriped pants right off Dustin's scrawny body.

The gum lost its flavor quickly. Dustin spat it into the trash can and headed back to the table. He wasn't hungry and knew he wouldn't finish his meal. He only hoped Gordon wouldn't pressure him into ordering dessert, because he wouldn't be able to say no, and he could only imagine himself throwing up some kind of designer cheesecake into Terrell Briggs's lap.

"It makes a statement," Gordon was saying. "No one messes with you, but there's always someone down the line, maybe even one of your friends, who thinks he can do better." Gordon waved a finger at Terrell. "So all I'm saying is, you need to back this personal power you got, this image, with some real firepower."

Dustin felt something squeezing the inside of his chest as he listened. Gordon had never spoken to *him* in the same respectful tone. And he heard more than just respect for Briggs—it was that the respect seemed to be understood, accepted, and unquestioned from the beginning. The squeezing in Dustin's chest grew tighter. Gordon had never shown that kind of confidence in *him*. Now Briggs turned and eyed Dustin as Gordon spoke, and then slowly turned away again. It was as though Dustin were a fly buzzing against the window, a momentary distraction but nothing of worthy of Briggs's attention.

"And that's what makes you solid," Gordon was saying. "That's what makes you the one everyone else looks up to. I'm talking about *power*."

Another thought invaded Dustin's mind: He had

heard this speech of Gordon's before, when they had set up business in Chicago. Gordon set up exclusive "contracts" with the most powerful gang in an area, then saw to it the gang remained the most powerful. If a rival gang arrived with semiautomatic weapons, Gordon provided his customers with AK-47s, Russian-made machine guns. Dustin hated the speech. Gordon was kind to him, and generous, but sometimes Dustin would rather pretend he didn't know where Gordon got the money to pay him.

The two talked business for another ten minutes—well, really Gordon talked, with Terrell Briggs occasionally nodding, grunting, or throwing in a one-syllable word. They agreed on a time, on a place of delivery, then they shook hands. Gordon always shook hands after talking business; he'd often reminded Dustin that it fostered a good working relationship. He'd read so in a book once. Terrell took the offered hand, but Dustin sensed that, behind the man's stony, uneven face, he was laughing at the gesture.

Business was over. Gordon sat back in his chair and sipped at his wine. "So, your boys had to take care of a problem at Seabreeze," he said.

Terrell's eyes scanned the room, and Dustin had the feeling the man would have been more comfortable having this conversation in an alley at two A.M. "Yeah. We scared 'em off. They won't be back." With that, Terrell threw a final look of disdain at Dustin and left the table.

Gordon's index finger tapped the table sharply. In a mental echo, Dustin heard Gordon say *I want 'em dead*

dead dead. He had given the order to Dustin. Had Dustin relayed these directions clearly to Terrell? He couldn't remember. And the lapse could land them in jail. They were all stuck in this together now: In demonstrating the use of the wand, another item Gordon wished to sell to Terrell, the two had joined interests in an unexpected way. The car trick they pulled had helped both of them. It had gotten Carla locked up, which was Gordon's wish, and when the old man, Underwood, died, it had disposed of Terrell's problem. Now they all had a stake in the secret, and if those kids weren't dead, it was Dustin's fault. Gordon had delivered the order to *him.* Dustin lifted his glass of water and sipped from it.

"And Dustin," said Gordon, "your job was to watch my other concern. Any problems?"

The glass danced a little jig in Dustin's fingers. He caught it with both hands and returned it to the table, spilling a few drops. He toyed with the idea of lying, of telling Gordon no one had come to the police impound lot, no one had searched Carla Marcetti's car. But Gordon would know he was lying the same way Dustin's mother knew when Dustin lied about taking a dollar from her purse, or the way his teachers knew he was lying about cheating on a test. His lies seemed to write themselves across his forehead.

"Um, yeah, Gordon," he said. He didn't dare reach for the water again. "I caught the short kid, Ramiro, going through the glove compartment."

Gordon set his wineglass down slowly, twirling the

stem with his fingers so that the glass rotated—clockwise, counterclockwise, clockwise again.

"But I taught him a lesson, Gordon," said Dustin. "Put the gun you gave me right against his head. He won't be back; I'll tell you that much. And he didn't find anything neither, 'cause I woulda known. I woulda seen it."

Gordon said nothing. The glass, still moving, whispered against the tablecloth.

"Gordon," Dustin said, whining a little now, "I got confused, okay? First you say you want the kids dead dead dead—" Gordon raised a finger discreetly. Dustin's pleadings were a little too loud. "—and then you say we need Ramiro, that he's the reason Carla will keep her mouth shut. At the time, I didn't know what to do, you see? You always say be precise. But I don't know, sometimes you give me instructions, and it's like I'm reading a manual on how to connect a VCR or something."

Gordon raised his hand, a signal for Dustin to stop. "Enough," he said. "It's all right. I can't believe the Ramiro kid found anything at the impound lot, so as long as the other Malibu remains under water, we and Mr. Briggs have nothing to worry about." He propped his elbows on the table and linked his fingers together as though he were a father having a conversation about responsibility with his wayward son. "Dustin," he began, "we have two pieces of business to finish before I'll feel comfortable moving my organization here permanently. The first is taking care of our customer, Mr. Briggs. He's happy with our service so far. In three days, his order will arrive, and I wanna make sure he's still satisfied, understand?"

Dustin nodded. Gordon took another sip of wine and swiped his napkin across his lips. "The second piece of business is this: I wanna bury Carla Marcetti—either in the darkest cell in the penitentiary or under six feet of dirt. It makes no difference to me."

Seabreeze
Midnight

Seagulls. *Larus Californicus,* to be exact. Police forensic scientist Marco Weese heard them cawing, their cries loud *ahhhs!*

They're after the garbage, Weese thought. *Teenagers probably sneak in here late at night, holding private little picnics and leaving bits of hamburger bun or potato chips for the birds to find.* He waved at the two uniformed cops sent to accompany him and began his work.

In Weese's hand was a stainless steel dental pick, the same sort of tool a hygienist uses to scrape tartar from teeth. He let thoughts of the birds fade and concentrated again on the work before him. The old gate leading into the Seabreeze was made of chain link. The sharp tips of the links projected just a little past the steel bar that framed the gate, and while the projection was no more than a quarter inch, it was enough so any car that came roaring through might scratch its paint against the sharp tips.

Weese gripped his dental pick and studied those tips, squinting. Because Decker had called him at home, Weese was wearing his contact lenses. He wished instead for his work glasses, the ones with the black plastic frames and the length of surgical tubing that kept them from slipping off his face. He could see much better at night with those. Now, in the glare of the halogen lamp on its tripod behind him, Weese found the contacts made his eyes feel dry and tired.

And he was missing a documentary on the snowy egret. A beautiful bird! An extraordinary bird! Tape it indeed. Decker owed him for this.

Weese found tiny flecks of black clinging to the tips of the fence. With the dental tool, he scraped them into a circular plastic lab container about the size of his palm. The flecks were undoubtedly paint of some kind, though how important they might be, Weese could not say. He would have to wait until Decker gave him something with which to compare them. A car, for example.

The examiner turned his attention to the sandy lakeshore. Near some tire tracks were some glistening brass cartridges. *9mm*, Weese thought. *Bag 'em and tag 'em.* He then spotted some depressions in the wet sand. Obviously where the kids hunkered down, he thought. All around the depressions were perfectly straight lines. *And this is where the bullets scraped along the sand before burying themselves.* Digging along those lines, he found black pellets, their ends rounded and tipped like the nose cone of a rocket. He slipped them into a plastic evidence bag. *Clean bullets,* he thought with satisfaction. Tearing through the sand had not crumpled them into bits of lead slag, the way a ricochet off metal or bone might have. When Weese studied these under a microscope, the ballistics markings would be as clear as the lines on a sheet of notepaper.

Weese slipped the bag into his coat pocket. "Excellent," he said to himself. "It looks as though Decker might get his search warrant after all." He put away his tools, folding the lamps and tripods into leather cases. He put his equipment in the trunk of his car and slammed it shut.

The seagulls, startled by the sudden noise, shrieked their warnings to one another and fled across the water.

chapter
ten

dustin heard Gordon's roar—a great bellow, like an ox—followed by an explosion and the tinkling of glass. He kicked the covers off and drew himself into a seated position on the edge of the bed. He scratched his nose and, eyes finally open, drew himself to his feet and quickly changed into sweats and sneakers.

Gordon bellowed again. Dustin shivered.

In his groggy state, the stairs seemed to tilt down and away from him as he made his way to the kitchen. Dustin flattened his hands against his face and patted his cheeks to wake himself. He paused at the bottom step. Gordon's temper wasn't fading as fast as it usually did. Dustin heard his boss shouting obscenities at the walls and wondered what could have tripped the landmine in Gordon's head so early in the morning. What should he say when he got to the kitchen? A loud clattering followed the thought, and Dustin watched a kitchen chair fly into the living room and glance off the top of the dining table.

Silence for now, he decided, made the most sense.

He peeked around the corner into the kitchen. Gordon stood in robe and slippers, gripping a spatula in a way that reminded Dustin of a gang kid holding a switchblade. Gordon's face was shiny. The muscles in his neck looked strained and ropy beneath the skin. Something that at one time might have been an omelet sat in a frying pan on the stove, hissing and spitting and sending up a cloud of blue-gray smoke. In another pan lay slices of Canadian bacon, curled and blackened. A tremendous gold-brown stain made a circle on the wall, right about the height of Dustin's head. From there it ran down in wide rivulets, forming a dark puddle on the floor. Shards of broken glass, remnants of Mr. Coffee, floated in the puddle like miniature glass rowboats.

"You threw the coffee maker against the wall," said Dustin.

"I'm fine," said Gordon. The spatula wavered in his hand. "Have some breakfast." He smiled, a wide crack of a grin that seemed painted on. A small color television set rested on the kitchen counter. Gordon liked to hear the morning news as he made breakfast. Dustin's eyes went to the screen. He saw a man in a suit and tie, his expensive-looking shoes half-buried in wet sand.

"Well, it's not the kind of fish tale you tell your grandkids," said the reporter, "but it sure has local police interested. How did this automobile end up under several feet of water here at Seabreeze? It's a mystery—one the police are eager to solve. Now back to you, Marla..."

The picture shifted to a female anchorperson. Dustin heard her speak but couldn't really follow what she was saying. The television's speaker—or his mind—was fuzzy. "Have some breakfast," Gordon hissed. He flipped the charred omelet onto a plate, then a round slice of Canadian bacon, curled and hardened to the shape of a potato chip. Gordon shoved the plate at Dustin, who took it and held it dumbly.

Those kids, those Misfits, had found the car—the one that had actually killed the old man. Gordon had said it was one of his concerns, one of only two. And he had placed Dustin in charge of those concerns. Now Dustin understood why Gordon was angry, and he saw, finally, that *he* was the target of that anger.

"Gordon," said Dustin, "I'm sorry. I told Terrell to have his gang take care of these kids if they showed up at Seabreeze, but I can't remember if I told him the 'dead dead dead' part, you know? It was a simple mistake."

Robotlike, Gordon turned his back for an instant. Then he spun back around, a flash of something silver in his hand. Dustin had seen danger enough times to know it was coming now. He was already moving. He hurled his plate of food at Gordon. The hard omelet, still hot from the pan, burst against Gordon's cheeks and eyes. Gordon screamed, and the flash of silver spat flame. Dustin, sprinting for the back door, heard the *pffft* of another silenced gunshot and saw a little explosion of dust fall from the ceiling just ahead of him. He yanked the door open and ran, never pausing and never looking back. His feet pounded the sidewalk, powered by some internal motor. He dashed two miles, maybe three, before he noticed the ache in his lungs. He wondered what he would do now—in an unfamiliar town, away from anyone who knew him, away from Gordon—but the thought was there and gone, like the signs in the store windows Dustin passed. After a few moments in the warm spring sun, and with the bikini-clad girls smiling at him as he dashed by, he could almost forget why he was running. He even began to plan some: He would stay on the West Coast. The weather and bikinis had decided that. He would get away from Gordon. He'd go to San Diego, maybe tend bar in a beach club. *No regrets,* he reminded himself. Gordon had said that. He'd read it in a book once. Dustin did have one regret, though: He wished he had taken the ring. He really liked the ring.

3:20 P.M.
Bugle Point County Courthouse

A motion to dismiss.

Byte didn't fully understand what was technically involved with such a motion, but she understood this much: Cheryl Atterbury was asking a judge to release Mattie's mother from jail, and the district attorney was hem-hawing around trying to stop the judge from doing so. Byte also understood that this was not a trial. The jury and witness boxes were empty. She was hoping to see some stern, silent woman typing court transcripts into one of those odd devices that look like a cross between a typewriter and an antique adding machine, but she was disappointed in that respect as well. Even the judge seemed less formal than Byte expected. He leaned back in his chair and shifted as though he was crossing his legs. Right in the middle of the DA's argument, a courtroom clerk stepped behind the desk to deliver a mug of coffee to the judge, which he sipped while listening.

Peter, Byte, Jake, and Robin sat in the back of the courtroom. The mileage tag in Carla's car was not quite enough to force the DA to drop the charges against her. The car at the bottom of Seabreeze, by itself, was not sufficient. But together, Cheryl had suggested, the two pieces of evidence all but proved Carla Marcetti's innocence.

"And I was the last person to believe her," Byte whispered to Jake. "I didn't even want to give her a chance."

"In my chambers," said the judge. He and the two attorneys walked through a door and into the judge's private office.

Byte leaned toward Peter. "What do you think they're going to talk about back there?"

"I think it means he's going to yell at one of them," said Peter, "and he doesn't want anyone else to hear."

Jake put his arm across Byte's shoulder as though it had been there a thousand times before. When he spoke, his mouth came close, tickling her ear. "How's Mattie?" he asked. Mattie had come with them, but he had refused to join them in the courtroom. Instead, he had chosen to wait three blocks away, sitting on the blacktop, his back against the stucco wall of the county jail building. He'd said he needed quiet and time to think, and he wanted to think *there*. Byte wondered if he wanted to be in its shadow as he thought about his mother and the events of the last few days.

"I better check on him," she said.

She went out through the heavy swinging door at the back of the courtroom. A flight of stairs led her to the courthouse lobby and into the achingly bright sunlight outside. If she shielded her eyes and crinkled her nose to set her glasses straight, she could just make out a tiny figure sitting on the steps near the jailhouse entrance.

He remained silent when she walked up and sat next to him. He had drawn his legs up and wrapped his arms around them, resting his chin on his knees. Byte assumed the same posture and waited for him to say something first.

"How does it look?" he finally asked.

"Good," said Byte. "Cheryl looks confident, and the DA doesn't have much to say. He just shouts out legal phrases in Latin that I don't understand. I could see the spit flying from his mouth." She inched closer to Mattie. "You don't think you should be in there?"

He didn't answer.

"You know," Byte said quietly, "when my dad died, it was so hard. I was a mess. My mom was a mess." Mattie didn't answer. He seemed so small, she felt she could almost hold him in her lap. "I was still really mad at him, you know? For leaving us. It was like he had deliberately abandoned us. For a while I went to a therapist. Even now I think—well, he's not going to be there to take pictures of me for my senior prom, or walk me down the aisle when I get married, and I still get mad."

Mattie's voice was soft. "But he didn't choose to abandon you," he said. "He was in a car accident, right?"

"Yeah," said Byte. "And common sense would tell you that it should make a difference, but it doesn't. In my head I know it was an accident, but it's like this voice in me keeps saying, 'Yeah, but if he *really* loved you, he'd have been more careful.' I guess when you're little, you don't think anything happens by chance. Your parents seem so much in control; accidents don't happen to them."

"I didn't lose my mom because of an accident," Mattie pointed out. "She *chose* to leave me with my grandparents. She knew where I lived, but she *chose* not to write or call. She could have gotten a regular job, but she *chose* to involve herself in…" His voice had been growing louder, but now it trailed off. He picked up a twig that was lying on the step and cracked it between his fingers. "And you're saying I should just make up with her?"

"I'm saying you have a chance to make up with her," said Byte. "I know it isn't my place to tell you what to do…I don't know what it feels like to be in your position right now. But you can be the grown-up here, even if she spent a long time *not* being a grown-up. What if she were to vanish off the face of the earth right now, like my dad did? Wouldn't you regret—maybe, just a little bit— not getting to know her? I just think you should consider it, 'cause from my perspective you're lucky to *have* the chance."

Mattie had not turned to her once during the conversation. He had stared forward, his eyes locked on something distant. Now Byte realized what he was seeing, the mural on the wall of the convenience store across the street. She studied it now—the young Latina bathed in a heavenly light, holding a baby in her arms and gazing down at it through stylish sunglasses.

"What do you think it means?" Mattie asked.

Byte suddenly flashed on an image of her father. She was four years old, clinging to his leg, hiding behind him as he held up their new kitten for her to pet. In her mind she couldn't see his face; he was all legs, a shiny belt buckle, huge hands, gentle voice. She felt her eyes starting to burn.

"I think," she said, "it means that God watches out for single mothers."

Lieutenant Decker crouched near the steel-door entrance to the building, arm extended, weapon ready, a crackle of voices in his earpiece. Three other officers slipped alongside to join him. Sam, Decker's partner, held a shotgun; others nervously gripped an iron battering ram.

"Team Three ready!" Decker whispered.

The building was the size of a small warehouse. Its corrugated steel wall was hot against Decker's shoulder. He grimaced and rotated his arm, relieving an itch under his Kevlar vest. Marco had come through again. The bullets found at Seabreeze matched those found at a robbery scene two years ago—a robbery Terrell Briggs was accused of committing. It wasn't enough for an arrest warrant, since Briggs hadn't been convicted, but the possible link, along with the fact that Terrell's car matched the Misfits' description of the black sedan at Seabreeze, was enough to get a search warrant. Decker had watched Terrell Briggs come and go from this building for two days. Briggs was inside now, Decker knew, and was undoubtedly armed. Members of the BPPD's gang unit, auto theft task force, and robbery division—sixteen officers in all—waited for a signal.

Decker's earpiece crackled again. *Go!*

Decker jabbed his finger—*now!*—and the battering ram crashed against the door like a cannon shot. The steel caved inward, sending up a shower of hardware—springs, bits of lock, a doorknob that clanged when it hit the concrete. Doors on the building's other three walls burst in at the same second. The commands of the officers echoed sharply, like ricochets: "Police!" "Get down!" "Hands behind your head!" Music pounded inside the warehouse, adding to the noise.

Six members of Terrell's gang dove for the floor. A seventh, who couldn't have been more than thirteen years old, saw the officers coming at him from three directions and so turned his back and ran—right into the arms of the fourth group. Officers patted down the gang, removed three handguns and a Phillipine butterfly knife, and handcuffed the whole group.

Decker approached Terrell Briggs. The man stood shirtless in front of a black sedan. Decker could see a four-inch scar across Briggs's shoulder, an old knife wound that looked as though no doctor had ever treated it. Briggs's left cheekbone, higher and larger than the right, gave his face an uneven look that made Decker want to angle his head slightly to straighten out the picture.

Decker showed Briggs a sheet of paper bearing a judge's signature. "Terrell Briggs, we have a warrant to search the premises. Take a seat against the wall."

Before he could begin his search, however, Decker had to deal with an annoyance. The hood and both doors of the sedan were splayed open so that it looked a little like a wounded blackbird. Music pounded from the CD player inside. Decker reached in, pushed the eject button, and tossed the CD onto the passenger seat. Sam raised a questioning eyebrow.

"I hate rap," Decker explained. He started to close the car door, but something caught his attention. "Hey, what's this?" Three fine scratches, perfectly straight and perfectly parallel, ran along the length of the car from the fender to the rear end. Decker studied them a moment, then stood to face Terrell Briggs. "What happened to your ride, Terrell? You been driving through chain-link fences?" Briggs said nothing.

"Hey, Marv," said Sam, "check this out." Sam was holding up a can. "Touch-up paint."

"Ah, I see," said Decker. "You're running your own personal body shop, right Terrell?" Again no answer. "All right," said Decker. "Take them outside for questioning while we look around in here." With the gang members gone, the team spent forty minutes searching the place. Aluminum cans littered the floor of the small warehouse and several posters decorated the walls—though no one had seemed to figure out how to tape them so that all four corners would stay up. Oil stains marred the concrete. A beat-up wooden desk sat in one corner, a lop-sided chair behind it. The computer on top of the desk, though, with its flat screen monitor, was black and sleek and clearly newer and faster than anything the PD would buy.

"Hey, Ma, look what followed me home," said Sam. "Can I keep it?"

Decker snorted. "Yeah, I wouldn't mind having one too. What do you suppose these jokers need it for?" He eyed the device for a long moment. A cable snaked from the back of the computer to a customized printer. Feeding the printer was a thick roll of—not paper—but some sort of sheet plastic. What *did* these jokers need it for?

"Lieutenant?" called a voice. Decker turned to the sound and saw a uniformed cop holding up what looked like an open briefcase. Inside the case, fitted into velvet-lined compartments, were the disassembled parts of an automatic assault rifle.

"That's all we need," Decker said. "Read 'em their rights."

"Oh, and Lieutenant," said the officer, "what do you want me to do with this? I found it on the table over there." He was holding some kind of black wand about ten inches long and as thick around as a flashlight. A tube of red glass lined one edge.

Decker shrugged. "I dunno," he said. "Just bag it like everything else."

The police interrogation room was meant to feel cold and intimidating. The chairs were steel, their backrests angled so that you had to sit just so to keep the metal from digging into your shoulder blades. The table was a cheap and ugly piece of furniture, but it made a satisfying echo when Decker pounded it with the flat of his hand. The walls were white, coated with shiny paint that glared with reflected light and tired the eyes.

Terrell Briggs sat in one of the steel chairs, his legs crossed and one arm slung over another chair's back as though he were at the movies and his girlfriend was sitting next to him. He slouched nonchalantly, which tempted Decker to swat the backside of Terrell's head to get his attention. Briggs had already brought in his attorney.

"Here's what we have," Decker said. "We have paint flecks taken off the fence at Seabreeze, flecks that just happen to match the paint on your car, Terrell. We have fresh scratches on the car itself, scratches that exactly match the spacing between the chain links. We have bullets dug out of the sand. We're doing more ballistics tests now, but I'm betting they came from one or more of the guns we just confiscated from your little private garage. Bottom line, Terrell—you're going to jail for attempted murder."

Briggs's attorney was a short man with a bald head, a bit of a paunch, and the thick neck and jowly cheeks of a bulldog. He let his briefcase bang against the tabletop as he set it down. "Cut the nonsense, Lieutenant," he said. "Unless you match those bullets to a gun, you have nothing more than an illegal weapons charge against my client."

Decker shrugged. "Then I guess your *client* has nothing to worry about until tomorrow." He turned to Briggs, who was smiling a smile that gave Decker the impression the gang leader had fangs. "In the meantime, Terrell, you might want to consider the fact that we also have the car we pulled out of the water at Seabreeze. You better hope we don't connect you to it, because if we do, and if that's the car that killed Joseph Underwood, the charge won't be attempted murder. It'll be murder one."

Briggs's enlarged cheekbone made the eye above it appear smaller than the other. The lieutenant caught a flicker in that eye, as though the mind behind it were calculating. He focused on it, refusing to turn away.

Peter dropped the cardboard box onto Sam's desk with a loud *ooof*. "Is this okay?" he asked.

"That'll work," said Sam.

When Peter heard that Decker would be part of a raid against Terrell Briggs and his gang, he had asked the lieutenant if the Misfits could follow along. Decker had spun him around and pushed him toward the door. Peter had next suggested a compromise: The Misfits could wait outside and join the search team after the danger was over. Decker told him to go home or he'd have to shoot him. Ultimately, Peter felt like a grounded kid who had to wait for his friends to come home from a party so he could hear about it. The Misfits were in the lieutenant's office now, surrounded by boxes filled with evidence bags—like the freezer bags Peter's mother used for leftovers—full of notebooks, floppy diskettes, money, the occasional handgun, even a half-eaten cheeseburger.

Peter held up the burger bag. "Gonna dust this for fin-gerprints?" he asked.

"Nah," said Sam, grabbing it. "It's mine. I just wanted it to stay fresh."

Jake and Mattie sat on the floor with their backs against the lieutenant's desk, a large cardboard box between them. Jake reached into the box every so often to lift up one of the evidence bags and hold it to the light, then returned it to the box unless Mattie asked to see it too. Robin sat down next to Peter and picked up a bag containing floppy disks. The labels on the disks, smeared by grease stains and finger smudges, bore only a range of dates written in black marker—2/4–2/18, 3/11–3/25. "We need to see what's on these," she whispered. She turned toward Sam, and her smile flickered on. "Could you show me where the restrooms are?" she asked. "It's so easy to get lost in this building."

"Sure," said Sam. He stood and headed toward the door with Robin following. Just before stepping into the hallway, he stopped and pointed his burger at the remaining Misfits. "Do *not* touch that evidence," he said. "It still needs to be logged in."

The moment he was gone Byte grabbed a pair of latex

surgical gloves from Sam's desk and pulled them on—to avoid leaving her own fingerprints on the evidence, and to keep from spoiling someone else's prints. In seconds she had the cables attached to Terrell Briggs's computer. "I've been dying to play with this thing," she said.

Mattie laughed in disbelief. "I can't believe you're doing that!"

"Look at this way," said Byte. "What's going to happen the moment he comes back? Someone else will read the files, only we won't get all the details, right?"

"Hey," said Jake, "what's this?"

He was holding another baggie, this one containing an object the length and width of a large flashlight. It was black, with switches on the side and a red glass tube along one edge. Peter hadn't a clue what it was, which of course meant he now had an overpowering urge to find out.

Mattie took the bag from Jake's fingers. Through the plastic, he touched one of the switches and the wand began to hum. The glass tube became a neon red streak. "Hey!" Mattie said, "I bet I know what this is! It's a scanner."

The computer's welcome tone chimed. Byte had already powered it up. "That little thing?" she asked. "Cool. I've seen pictures in catalogs, but never one up close. You run it along a photo or a document, and it digitizes it."

"It's a hand-held model," said Mattie, "to use with a laptop, I guess."

"Let's see it," said Byte. Peter noted that she hadn't bothered to ask permission for this either, and he was surprised at how much he liked her for it. She connected the scanner to a port in the back of the computer and selected some commands with the mouse. Peter and the others gathered around her, watching. After a moment, an image began to form on the screen, blurry at first, then becoming clearer as detail layered upon detail. Peter saw letters and numbers in cobalt blue and the word "California" spelled proudly at the top.

Byte canted her head. "It's a license plate," she whispered.

"Yes," Peter agreed. He pulled on a glove and reached for one of the floppy diskettes. "Now try this."

The diskette contained four files, and like the one that remained in the scanner's memory, each appeared to be a digital image of a license plate. Byte called them to the screen one at a time.

Mattie pointed. "Wait, that's my mom's! What's going on here?"

"Hit Print," Peter suggested.

Clicking noises came from Briggs's odd-looking printer, followed by a hum as it engaged. It spat out the sheet plastic in a series of slow jerks.

Byte threw a glance at the door. "Geez, these dopes spent a fortune on a top of the line computer, you'd think they'd spring for a faster printer."

"Well, we're all going to get our heads bitten off if it doesn't finish before Sam gets back," added Jake.

The sheet of white plastic finally lurched through, emblazoned now with a full-sized, and quite perfect, image of a California license plate. Jake snipped it off with a pair of scissors when it finished.

"It's brilliant," Peter said. "What's the problem with stealing a car? The owner reports it stolen. The police are on the lookout for a car with the owner's license plate. But what if you find another car just like the one you want to steal? The same make, model and color. You scan its license plate and print it on a sheet of plastic. Sure, it's not metal, but who's going to look that closely? Then you go out and steal the kind of car you want. You take off the real license plate and replace it with the one you copied."

Byte finished for him. "So then the thief is driving around in a stolen car that was *never reported stolen*. If someone checks out the license plate, everything matches up."

A voice shouted from the doorway. *"What do you think you're doing?"* Peter's face flushed, and he saw Byte cringe. She moved hurriedly as if to shut down the computer, but then seemed to realize it was too late. They'd been caught. Sam and Robin stood together in the doorway, Robin shifting uncomfortably.

"Sorry," she said. "I didn't think the bathroom would be so close."

"Sam, hold on," said Jake. "Before you get mad, look at this." He pointed to the computer screen and explained what the Misfits had found and what they thought it meant. "Think of what these guys could get away with," he said. "They'd be able to rob a convenience store in a stolen car, then just sit back while the person who really owns the car with that license plate takes the blame."

Mattie tapped the screen, where the numbers of Carla

Marcetti's license plate sat bright and clear. "Or they could kill an old man and set up an innocent woman to take the fall," he said.

"We know that Mr. Underwood caused problems for Terrell," said Peter. "What if this scanner rig and the printer that prints on plastic make up another one of Gordon Moxley's 'services'? Maybe he's trying to sell it to Briggs."

"And maybe using it to frame Carla and get rid of Mr. Underwood," Jake said, "was a way of testing it, or showing it off. Kind of like some sick sort of…infomercial."

Sam tossed his burger to the desk. A slice of tomato slipped out and landed on some papers, but he didn't seem to notice. "I'd better tell Decker," he said.

Terrell Briggs had been listening to this cop, Decker, spout off for about half an hour. He heard the evidence against him. He heard Decker's promises of jail time. Through it all, he had remained silent, speaking only when it came time to ask to make his phone call, and then he had just muttered "Gimme a phone." He'd written off Decker as fat and old—a lazy, donut- and french fry–scarfing, pastrami-on-rye-and-extra-mayo cop. The kind who'd be dead in a week if assigned real street duty. But while staring Terrell down, the cop had casually rolled up the sleeves of his shirt, revealing thick forearms, solid muscle moving underneath. Decker's fingernails were clipped to the nubs, the hands white and scrubbed clean, but the meat of his palms and the fleshy part of his fingers were hard and calloused. Terrell could see a gun fitting comfortably in a hand like that.

The cop's partner came to the door and tapped on the glass. Decker stepped outside and the two huddled together, whispering. A moment later the detective came back, closing the door so that it barely clicked when it shut.

"Remember what I said a while ago, Terrell? About murder one?" The cop sat on the corner of the table, looking like a father about to explain all the world's truths to his troubled son. "I think maybe we can forget that. I'm thinking I can recommend to the DA that the charge be lowered to murder two."

"What's this about, Lieutenant?" asked the attorney. Decker continued looking directly at his suspect and ignored the attorney. Terrell respected that.

"Do you know why I'm making that recommendation, Terrell?" the lieutenant asked. "Do you know why I'm willing to do a favor for a guy who oughta be shoveling dirt in San Quentin?" He leaned forward, planting those thick hands on the table in front of Terrell. His nose came within inches of Terrell's face. "It's because you're going to do *me* a favor. You're going to tell me everything you know about a man named Gordon Moxley—down to the smell of his breath and the last pimple on his nose."

chapter eleven

The following day...

gordon Moxley sat alone in his townhouse, his weight sinking into an overstuffed chair. The arms and back of it loomed around him, and the seat seemed unusually high. He had the odd feeling that his feet were dangling, that they wouldn't quite reach the floor, but when he checked they were resting on the carpet.

He stared forward, his cell phone in his hand. Without looking, he punched a speed dial button and held the phone to his ear. It rang six, seven, eight times before he gave up. Mom had caller ID.

His operation was a shambles. Worse than a shambles—a wreckage. Gordon could not be precisely sure how it had happened, but an hour ago Chicago police had burst in on his weapons supplier, arresting more than a dozen people and seizing all of the AK-47s set aside for Terrell Briggs. Gordon had ordered the weapons based on Terrell's ability to pay for them, and now Briggs himself was under arrest, not to mention the thugs in his gang. The debt, the obligation, fell to Gordon, and Gordon couldn't pay, for he'd discovered hours ago that his bank accounts had been frozen by court order. The situation was worse than a disaster. According to the morning news, the police in Bugle Point were looking for him. But that was nothing. He had lost his credibility with his clients. His supplier in Chicago no doubt wanted to kill him. And the worst insult—Gordon had caught it, too, on the local news— was that a judge had freed Carla Marcetti.

He hit the redial button on the phone, letting the device rest in his lap instead of holding it to his ear. He could hear its ghostly ring, vague and very far away, over and over. The anger welled up inside him again. He conquered the urge to hurl the phone across the room and laid it instead on the table in front of him.

Gordon glanced around the townhouse. He had waited until last night to clean up the coffee-stained wall and burnt food he'd left in the kitchen. Only the bullet holes in the wall and ceiling remained. Gordon, his face stinging from the hot food Dustin had thrown, had continued firing even after Dustin ran off. He had emptied the clip, shooting until the light, compressed-air sound of the silencer became the metallic clicking of an empty gun. Gordon actually felt a tinge of regret over what had happened. He had gone over the fight in his mind countless times. Oh, Dustin had to be punished for his stupidity. But perhaps, Gordon thought, he had gone too far. Perhaps Dustin's mistakes were partly

Gordon's fault. He may have given Dustin too much responsibility, pushing the boy beyond his limits. Dustin, at twenty-two, was just that—a boy. The stupid clothes he wore, the stupid ring he'd bought, should have been a message to Gordon. Dustin wasn't ready for a man's work.

The urge to throw something was almost unbearable. *No! Do not get angry!* he reminded himself. He had to remain calm. It was easy to explode, to let the temper come over him like a thunderstorm, but he could not afford to lose control now. The police had the car that had killed the old man. They had Terrell. They'd *released* Carla. Enough information sat rotting in the heads of those two to send Gordon to jail for a very long time. Gordon wasn't worried about Terrell. Terrell had been driving the car that had killed Joseph Underwood. The gang leader had a healthy interest in remaining silent. But Carla…Gordon felt a flash of his old love for her—and hated her all the more now that she'd betrayed him. Dustin had only been an idiot. Gordon could forgive that in time, but he could not forgive Carla's betrayal.

The anger rushed over him in spite of his efforts to hold it back. Gordon rose and paced the room. *Calm, calm,* he told himself, but he was beyond that now. His hatred of Carla grew, churning like an approaching hurricane, black clouds roiling inside him. He had nothing now. No organization, no money, *nothing.* Now he knew he would kill Carla Marcetti. He would do so with his own hands. He had made a promise to her in the court-room where she'd betrayed him, and now he would keep that promise.

Gordon reached again for his cell phone. He had no organization, but he still had a single "friend" in Bugle Point. She had needed money, and Gordon had given it to her in exchange for information. Now she likely had an even bigger need for money. Gordon still had five thousand dollars in cash. He wanted to find Carla Marcetti. For five hundred bucks, he was pretty sure the woman would do the work for him. A cracking sound came from his fist. He had been squeezing the cell phone. Cursing himself, he pushed the Talk button and held the phone to his ear.

It still worked.

Later...

Mattie sat in the back seat of Jake's Escort, pressed between Peter and Robin and feeling a little like a piece of baloney between slices of bread. Grimacing, he leaned forward and adjusted the rearview mirror so he could see himself. His hair was slicked down with what he now knew was too much gel. Even so, his cowlick stood up a bit at the back of his head, curling up from the rest of his hair and refusing to lie flat. Mattie patted it down, but it sprang up just like before.

"You look fine," Robin said. "Quit stressing."

"Yeah," Peter agreed. "I don't think I've ever seen you so dressed up."

Mattie stared down at his navy blue slacks and white, long-sleeved, button-down shirt. The truth was, he hadn't wanted to look dressed up. Earlier, as he had showered and scrubbed his teeth and slathered on deodorant, a voice inside him had told him to slow down, to think. Wear jeans, the voice said, the ones with the holes in the knees. Wear your favorite T-shirt. The big sneakers with the neon-green tubing in the heel are more comfortable than those wing-tipped loafers, the voice insisted. Mattie suspected the voice was right. His casual clothes would have sent a clearer message about who he was. And more significantly, they would have proclaimed that a meeting with his mother wasn't all that important, that Carla Marcetti did not merit the extra trouble of ironing a pair of navy blue slacks.

Still, he'd found himself reaching for the fancy clothes, the black dress socks he never wore, the shoes that pinched his feet.

He licked his palm and pressed down again on his hair. The cowlick sprang back up.

Jake looked at him in the mirror as he drove. "So what do you think you'll talk about?" he asked.

Nothing. Everything. "I don't know," Mattie said.

Five minutes passed. No one spoke. Mattie tugged at collar of his shirt, which was digging into his neck. "Um, look, can we just talk?" he asked.

"Talk?" asked Byte.

"Yeah," said Mattie, "*talk.* You're so quiet. And when you do talk, you whisper, and you have this tone like everything is so serious. Just stop it, okay? I feel like someone who's lying in a hospital bed, and you've all gathered around to watch me die. I can't stand it."

Jake shrugged. "Fine. I'll talk about whatever you want to talk about," he said. "Just don't ask me to let you play with my tuner anymore."

"Okay," said Mattie.

"Well, you pick," said Robin. "What do you want to talk about?"

Mattie considered the question. "Someone make fun of me," he said.

"Huh?" said Byte. "We all said you looked nice. We're just not used to seeing you all dressed up. But there's nothing to make *fun* of—"

"No," said Mattie. "I mean it. Someone make fun of me. Right now."

"Okay," Jake offered. "You look like Alfalfa in the Little Rascals."

Mattie nodded, mollified. "Thank you," he said. "I feel better now. And thanks for dropping me off."

"Anytime," said Jake. "It was worth it just to see you wearing wing-tips."

Jake pulled the car into the parking lot of Maggio's, Mattie's favorite Italian restaurant. Carla Marcetti had wanted to take Mattie to dinner, and she had insisted Mattie choose the place. Maggio's was generally loud and packed, and an old singer Mattie knew would be performing tonight, which meant Mattie would have plenty of distractions if he needed them. If he and his mother wanted to steal off to a corner and talk about…everything…they could. And if they decided to talk about nothing—well, the general commotion in Maggio's would allow that too.

Mattie sucked in a breath. He saw her.

Carla Marcetti walked from her car to the front of the restaurant, where she paused and looked out over the parking lot. She wore a dark skirt and a white blouse, and she had curled her hair. She clutched a purse in front of her. In the light over the restaurant door, she looked delicate, fawnlike, almost…

"Your mom's pretty," Robin said.

Mattie kept his thoughts to himself. "Don't go anywhere," he whispered.

"We'll be right across the street at Taco Tio," Peter answered. "We're close if you need us."

Byte opened the passenger door and stepped out, pulling the seatback forward. Robin then climbed out of the back seat so Mattie could get out too. The two girls gave him a hug. "Be the grown-up," Byte said.

Mattie started to nod but stopped himself. "Maybe," he said.

He headed, very slowly, toward the entrance to the restaurant. As he drew closer, his mother fidgeted. She let one hand go from the purse, and the purse wavered a bit. Her arms separated as though to hug Mattie, then dropped to her sides when he moved no closer. The shadows around her eyes were gone, he noticed. She was wearing perfume. Her arms were thin and pale.

"Want to go in?" she asked.

Her name was Rhonda. She had no children. She was unmarried. Her boyfriend had recently dumped her. She'd been turned down for membership at the gym for bad credit. And as of a few days from now, she would no longer be a guard at the Bugle Point County Jail. Now she could say she truly had nothing. And yes, it was her own fault, she knew—for she had made her own choices—but a large share of the blame also rested on the shoulders of a guy she had seen only a few times. His name was Gordon Moxley.

Rhonda thought of these things as she sat in a rented car at the far end of Maggio's parking lot. She saw the Ramiro kid and his mother meet at the door and go in. She had been following Carla Marcetti for two hours. It had taken a while to track her down; apparently she had been avoiding her apartment since her release from jail. Rhonda stared at the cell phone on the seat next to her. Moxley was waiting for her call.

The way Moxley had come on to her in Brannigan's had caught her off guard. Rhonda occasionally liked to stop off at the bar after work and have a few drinks with her girlfriends. One night a few weeks ago a man with long, dark hair had come up to her, chatting innocently, making her laugh, listening sympathetically when she dumped on him the whole story of the evil ex-boyfriend. The evening wore on and on, and she stayed in Brannigan's far later than she normally would have—and told him far more about herself than she would have told any other stranger. He liked her—it was so obvious. He came back every night for a week. And these informal dates with him grew later and later.

One evening, as midnight approached, he began telling her the story of *his* ex-girlfriend. Carla Marcetti. Yes, they had broken up, but he was still a concerned friend. He knew he was asking a huge favor, he said, but could Rhonda just sort of keep an eye and an ear open for him while Carla was in the county jail? Of course, he would never ask Rhonda to do anything wrong. Just tell him who came in to see Carla, what was said behind closed doors, what were her chances of an acquittal. He was just *concerned*. And because he knew this would inconvenience Rhonda, he would compensate her—well—for every piece of information. It was the money that should have told her something was wrong, but the guy would smile or crack a joke when he handed it to her, maybe kiss her on the cheek, and her concerns would vanish. The smart thing, Rhonda now understood, would have been to report Moxley the moment he had approached her. But she had agreed to help, and now, because of him, she had nothing. That detective—Decker—had been snooping around the jail, wanting to know who had been on duty when those kids were there. Who knew their names? he had asked. How many people had seen the emblem on their business card? Soon he would have his answers, and Rhonda would lose her job. Gordon Moxley was a chain twisting tighter and tighter around her neck.

And now he had offered her five hundred dollars to do one final favor. He was too hot with the police now. He couldn't follow Carla, but Rhonda could. She could tail Carla for an afternoon and wait until just the right moment to pick up the phone. The timing had to be right, Gordon had insisted. Rhonda, against her instincts, had said yes. She had no choice. She needed the money. And now she was more of a prisoner than Carla Marcetti had ever been.

Rhonda swallowed. The woman had her kid with her.

She was supposed to call Gordon Moxley now. It was a simple thing to do, to pick up a phone and punch in a few numbers, say a few words. But she remembered the sound of Moxley's voice when he'd called earlier. He had spoken quietly, without a hint of anger, but Rhonda had shuddered all the same. The voice was a whisper, a shadow, a tap on the shoulder from a ghost.

All she had to do, the voice had said, was tail Carla Marcetti for one night. Call him after dark. Tell him where she was.

He would handle the rest.

The phone felt cold in her hand. Five hundred dollars just for watching, waiting, and making a phone call. Moxley terrified her, but he had never lied to her, never cheated her, and always forked over the cash he promised. She *would* call. She *had* to call. She needed the money. She didn't really know, for sure, what Gordon was going to do. He hadn't told her. So it wasn't like it was her fault if anything happened to Carla Marcetti.

Five hundred dollars. She picked up the cell phone and dialed the number. A voice whispered "Yeah?"

"They're both at Maggio's restaurant," said Rhonda. "They've just gone in."

"Good," said Gordon. "I need you to wait ten minutes, then do one more thing for me…"

The ghost touched her shoulder again, and again she shuddered.

The restaurant was packed…and loud. Servers bustled between the red-and-white checked tablecloths. Having a serious talk in this too-bright setting would be like having one at a carnival with clowns and whirling rides and clanging and laughing and music all around.

"Wow," said Mattie. "We'll be lucky to get a table."

"Not a problem," said Carla. "I made a reservation."

She had made reservations—at Maggio's, where reservations were rarely necessary. Apparently she had taken no chances. Mattie had chosen this restaurant, and she hadn't wanted to disappoint him. Mattie felt a small rush of affection for Carla for her effort. It wasn't love, more like the distant warmth you might feel for a stranger who gives you change for a payphone.

The hostess led them through the crowded tables toward the nicest one in the restaurant, a corner table near some potted trees and plants and a small, trickling fountain. Mattie's opened menu was nearly the size of a newspaper. He hid himself behind it and looked at all the items that usually made his mouth drool. Cannoli. Chicken cacciatore. Fettuccini. Tonight none of them sparked his appetite. The thought of moist, heavy pasta made his stomach churn. As minutes passed, even his glass of water sat untouched, beaded with condensation. He peered over his menu at his mother. She wasn't studying hers at all. She was just staring at him, a pained, pleading look in her eyes.

"Have you decided what you want?" she asked.

Mattie shook his head and hid himself again. Only then did he realize that his mother might have meant the question in an entirely different way than he had just taken it. "I'm still thinking," he said.

Carla smiled. "Take your time."

A shadow fell over the table—Celia, the waitress, stout in her Italian-peasant uniform, arrived with her order pad. The pen, for some reason, remained in her pocket. "Ms. Marcetti?" she asked. "You have a phone call."

Carla frowned and rose slowly from the table. Mattie could almost see her running her day through her mind, asking herself if she had told anyone she was meeting her son here.

The table lamp flickered dark. Mattie tapped it, and it came back on again. "I'll be right back," Carla said. "I promise."

Carla approached the small cubicle off the restaurant's entrance. She could see the phone handset resting next to the cradle where the hostess had left it. Who could be calling her? The interruption had scrambled her emotions: annoyance at the call, relief at being alone for a moment, worry over Mattie. She wanted to thank the caller, then bite his or her head off.

"Hello?"

She heard a click and the dial tone, then immediately felt a painful jab in her hip. A hand clamped down over her mouth, and a voice hissed in her ear. "Hello, Carla," it said. "I'm here to keep my promise."

The room swirled around her. Her head filled with a fog that blurred everything—the door, some painting hanging on the wall, a potted plant. Hands gripped her shoulders and spun her around. A face framed in black hovered in front of her, wavering as though seen through a haze. The face was smiling. She saw fingers gripping a plastic tube that ended in a needle.

Gordon.

She fell against him. Felt him moving her through the door.

From where he sat, Mattie could see his mother standing in the cubbyhole where the phone was. Really, he could see a corner of her skirt, part of one shoulder, a bit of forearm. He returned to his menu.

His stomach, he discovered, was starting to settle. While he still couldn't focus on food—the menu seemed to be written in a language he didn't understand—he did find that the very idea of eating no longer made him feel woozy. He figured if he stared at the list of entrees long enough, something might even appeal to him. *Who'd a thunk it*, Mattie wondered. *Me, contemplating turning down a meal.*

He looked up again. The cubbyhole appeared empty. He frowned and laid his menu aside, scooting his chair from the table. He walked toward the cubbyhole in the same slow way he had approached his mother in front of the restaurant, hoping he didn't walk in on a personal call. The phone cradle sat on the tiny desk as it should. The handset hung by a tangle of curly wire. Carla Marcetti was gone.

Mattie shouldered his way through the door and into the parking lot. A black SUV idled near the front, the sound of its engine a loud purr. The tires shrieked as it tore away, and Mattie sprinted toward it. He caught just a glimpse of a light-haired woman in a white blouse in the passenger seat. Her head lolled against the window, rolling slightly with the vehicle's motion.

Mattie screamed. *"Mom!"*

As the SUV sped away, Mattie caught the bright lights just down the road—a neon sign of a little man in red wearing a giant yellow sombrero, the words Taco Tio blinking on, off, on, off…

Mattie raced toward it.

Robin held up her fork and studied the pinkish mass on it. "Don't you have to wonder about the person who first thought of refried beans?" she asked. "I mean, before he tried it, he actually had to think it was a good idea. Doesn't that strike you as being a little odd?"

"Nah," said Byte. "I wonder about the yogurt person. I mean, fruit and bacteria cultures, *yum.*"

"Hey, French people eat snails," added Jake.

Peter dropped his fork to his plate with a loud clatter. "Okay, I'm done," he said.

The door to the restaurant had opened perhaps five times since the Misfits had entered, and Peter had paid only scant attention to the people who walked in. When it burst open now, a gust of wind rushing in behind it, he turned to look.

It was Mattie.

He threaded a path between the tables so smoothly that, for a moment, he almost gave the impression he was walking *through* them. When he arrived at Byte's side, Peter could see Mattie's windblown hair and the heaving of his chest. Tears streamed down his face.

"Mattie?" said Byte.

The youngest Misfit huffed a few times, barely drawing in enough air to speak. "Someone…took my mom," he said. He laid one palm flat on the tabletop as he caught his breath. His other hand gripped the sleeve of Peter's shirt at the wrist, squeezing the fabric. "At the res…the restaurant."

"What?" said Byte.

"Who?" Jake asked. "Who took your mom? How?"

"A man," said Mattie. He was still sucking in huge

breaths. "A car…a big…SUV…" He pointed through the window and down the street, no doubt in the direction the car had gone.

"Did you see the driver?" asked Robin.

Mattie shook his head.

"Did you get a license number?" asked Jake.

Again, no.

"A license number probably wouldn't help us, all things considered," said Peter. "And besides, we don't need it. It's got to be Moxley. Terrell Briggs is in jail, and so is most of his gang, but…Mattie, what about the guy who held the gun on you in the impound lot?"

"I don't think so," Mattie said. "He let me go because I was Carla's son. So why would he go after her? It's got to be Moxley." He shook Peter's arm. "Peter, hurry! Think!"

Jake grabbed the cell phone from Peter's coat pocket and hit the speed dial button. "Lieutenant?" he said. Peter heard the speaker buzzing. "It's Jake. Listen, we need you to meet us at Maggio's restaurant right away. Someone—we're pretty sure it's Gordon Moxley—has kidnapped Mattie's mom." More buzzing. "Oh, and Lieutenant?" Jake added, "Make sure you bring your cell phone." He glanced at the others, apparently checking to make sure they agreed with what he was about to say. "'Cause I don't think we can wait for you there. We'll update you when we know more." He shut down the phone.

"Where do you suppose he took her?" Byte asked.

"Back to Seabreeze?" suggested Robin.

"It could be anywhere," said Peter. "His place, or out in the woods."

"Wait…wait…" said Jake. "Didn't Carla tell us that this Moxley guy had made some kind of specific threat? He told her exactly what he was going to do to her, right?"

"Yeah," Robin said. She squeezed her eyes shut. "Hold on. Wasn't it something about a tall building? I remember now…he told her he was going to drag her to the top of the tallest building he could find and throw her off. Those were Carla's exact words. She also said that he keeps his promises." Mattie's face turned gray. "Sorry," Robin said. "I wasn't thinking."

Peter shook his head. "The tallest building?" he asked. "Is that even possible? An office skyscraper will be closed at this hour, right? Moxley couldn't get in."

"An apartment building would be open," suggested Robin.

"Most big apartment buildings would have a doorman or security guard—or at least require some sort of pass code to get in," said Jake. "Moxley wouldn't be able to get inside one of those either."

"Briggs's warehouse was only one story tall," said Byte. "That's out."

"And if I remember right, Carla's apartment building is only three stories," added Robin. "That's out."

Peter shook his head. *It shouldn't be this hard,* he told himself, but all he could think to say was, "The projects, too. They're not tall enough."

Mattie had been lightly pounding his palm against the tabletop, hurrying the others, or growing angrier at the delay. Now Jake's hand came down on his, stopping the movement. A calm settled over the table, Jake at its center. Even Mattie quieted down. "I know where he's going," Jake said quietly. "He's going back to Eighth Avenue. He's taking her to the Skeleton Building."

eighth Avenue was still dark and spattered with graffiti and peeling paint, but the *sounds* of the street were different than Peter remembered. As Jake drove the Misfits down the block, a handful of children kicked a Hacky Sack back and forth, calling to each other in the glow of a street lamp. People cooled themselves on the front steps of their apartment buildings, sipping drinks, laughing, and occasionally shouting advice to one of the kids. Peter couldn't help noticing the change. People in the neighborhood seemed to feel safer now. Terrell Briggs and his gang were in jail. As the Misfits sped by, Peter saw that the primitive memorial for Mr. Underwood had grown larger, the flowers still fresh and piled high, as though they'd been replaced daily since the man's death. A sheet of plywood, whitewashed to form a clean background, bore a hand-lettered message in blue paint: Thank you, Joseph.

Jake drove on.

Just ahead, the Skeleton Building loomed over the street, a large full moon visible through its cagelike mesh of girders. In daylight the unfinished building was steel gray with patches of rust, but in the moonlight its girders became sharp black lines. The vertical beams spiked upward and seemed to grow taller as Jake's car approached. The Ford jerked to a stop across the street from the building, and the Misfits scrambled out.

"See the SUV, Mattie?" Peter called.

Mattie surveyed the road, shaking his head. "No. He's either not here, or he parked—"

"Oh, he's here," Byte said.

She was pointing high, at a far corner of the building. Peter saw a tiny flicker of movement, like the flutter of a moth's wings, black against the moon. He focused on the movement, and the movement became a shape—a man, half leading, half carrying a woman. She staggered, her knees collapsing, and he dragged to her to her feet.

Mattie made a little crying sound in his throat.

Peter reached into the pocket of his coat and took out his mother's cell phone. He tossed it to Robin. "Decker's already on his way to the restaurant," he said, "but call him again and tell him we've found Carla. His cell number's on the speed dial too."

"Gee," said Robin, "and what does *that* say about the kind of lives we lead?"

They ran to the base of the building, checking around its corners. Peter had hoped to find a builder's elevator, but he didn't see one.

"There's some scaffolding against the lower two floors," Jake said. He pointed at a network of steel pipes that looked remarkably like the rusty fire escapes on the apartment buildings down the block. Above the scaffold, there was only the steel grid and temporary floors of plywood. Each floor appeared to have a three-by-three-foot square cut into it. From the floor below, a rickety-looking ladder made of plywood and pine reached up into the opening.

"Someone could walk across the plywood sheets and go up the ladder to the floor above," Robin added. "See? The pattern repeats at each level."

Peter nodded. The Misfits would have to navigate these openings by moonlight and approach Gordon Moxley without being seen. "Hurry," Peter said. "Let's take one more look around the building and see if there's an easier way up."

They headed around what might be called a corner, a single massive girder that rose up and met with other girders to form right angles. Here the ground was hard, bare dirt, littered with scraps of lumber and rusty nails. Peter looked up and saw nothing but the platform marking the next floor ten feet above his head, and then another platform, and another. Any hopes he might have had of finding an easier path up the building crumbled like the clods of dirt under his feet. The scaffold, plainly, was the only way up. Moxley must have noted the same, dragging Carla with him onto the ladder and through the narrow opening. The Misfits had no choice; they would have to climb one dark, treacherous floor at a time.

"Aw, geez..." Byte cried out. "You guys, did anybody see where Mattie went?"

Why did the stupid building have to be so *tall*?

Mattie scrambled across the sheets of plywood that served as the third-story walkway. The sheets were nailed onto lengths of two-by-sixes, but over time, and with exposure to rain and sun, the layers of plywood had warped in places like the cover of an old paperback novel. One split as he stepped on it, crackling beneath his foot. Grasping, his hands found the wooden ladder that would take him to the next floor. He climbed it, then scurried across the platform to find the next ladder, and the next, until he was on the fifth level, the ground sinking away below him, a sea of black. From underneath him, he could just make out the creak of footsteps, a hiss of voices. His friends were following. *Can Moxley hear them?* Mattie wondered. *Can he hear me? And if he can...*

Maybe it helped that he couldn't see his mother as he climbed. The flooring came between him and the upper levels of the structure, so she seemed more distant to him, the danger to her less real. Then Mattie thought again of Gordon Moxley. He had never even seen a picture of the man, so the image that came to mind was monstrous. In his thoughts he heard a terrible laugh, saw black eyes and a wide, leering mouth with fangs. He shoved the thought away, but he couldn't hold back a moan. He reached for a length of two-by-four he found lying on the platform, taking it with him as a weapon. He found the next ladder, the one that would carry him to the sixth floor, and it shuddered even under his slight weight. Mattie looked out over the edge of the building at the distant ground—the tiny cars, the even tinier figures—and felt a dizziness come over him. He pitched forward, but his arm tightened around the ladder and held him there.

Angry at himself, a little growl rumbled in his throat and chest. *I hate heights,* he thought, and he reached for the next rung.

She was starting to come out of it.

Gordon wrestled Carla across the sixth-floor platform with both arms, one wrapped around her throat and the other around her waist. He was still half carrying her, but he could feel that her legs were bearing more of her weight, that they skittered in weak resistance now. She was starting to hold her head up instead of leaning it on his shoulder. He had quite intentionally used a low dose of the drug. He had not wanted to make her unconscious—too hard to move her, too obvious to anyone watching that something was wrong. Instead, he had wanted her disoriented, unaware, on her feet but incapable of fighting him. When they left the restaurant, she would have looked like a wife who'd had a little too much to drink. In the morning, when they found her body in the dirt below, he'd be long gone.

"Gordon," she mumbled, "no no no…"

At the sound of her voice—it had been so long since he'd heard it—he paused. He stopped dragging her and looked into her eyes, which were heavy-lidded, like those of someone coming out of a deep sleep. "Carla…?" he began.

Before he could think of something to say to her, she reached up with one hand and let it flop weakly against the side of his face. It felt as though she had tried to stroke his cheek, but then he realized that she had tried to slap him! In her weakness, she could only manage this dead, floppy fish gesture. The fact that she had wanted to hurt him filled him with a new rage. He grimaced, and his arms tightened around her. Her legs began to kick, and the point of a high heel jammed down on his instep. The jabbing sensation flared into a bright pain that he felt not only in his ankle but also in his stomach and behind his eyes. He grabbed her chin harshly, turned her to face him, and kissed her full on the lips. Then he took the chrome handgun from his pocket, with its yellowed ivory grips, and pressed the tip of its barrel against her temple.

"There," he said. "Now I can kill you."

As Mattie poked his head through the seventh-floor opening, he saw moving through the web of girders a terrible black shadow—two heads, arms flailing, a pair of legs rising and kicking wildly while another pair shuffled against the wooden platform, taking the figure closer and closer to the edge. Sounds came from the two-headed monster: a low grunting, as though from the effort of moving, along with a smothered crying. Mattie crept closer, and the sounds grew louder and overlapped. The man was speaking softly to Carla as he dragged her toward the edge of the building. Mattie couldn't make out the words, but the sound of the man's voice made his skin prickle. His mother's cries became louder and more insistent.

Mattie hid behind the girders, which stood like scattered pillars here and there across the platform. He moved from one to the next, drawing closer. When his mother grabbed one of the girders and wrapped her arms around it, the man gripped her wrists and yanked her toward the edge of the building. Mattie's fingers tightened around the two-by-four. He knew that Gordon Moxley intended to hurl his mother into space.

The man lifted Carla, but before Mattie could act, she reached out and found Gordon's face with her fingernails. Her hands dug in and raked downward, hard. The man yelled and fell to the floor. Carla might have gotten away then. She ran, but the man grabbed her ankle, and she tumbled to her knees. In an instant the man had his arms around her middle and was hauling her back to her feet, dragging her again to the edge.

Mattie stepped out from behind the girder, shouting. "Leave her alone!"

Surprised, the man turned. When he saw Mattie, he grinned, the bloody scratches on his face glistening in the moonlight. He let Carla drop to the floor, gripping her hand to keep her from escaping, and slowly raised the gun toward Mattie. "Bang bang, you're dead," he said.

Then he let out a scream. Carla had sunk her teeth into his hand.

Mattie swung the chunk of wood in a vicious arc, catching Moxley on the side of the face and jerking his head around viciously. Mattie swung his makeshift club harder, striking again and again, shouting every time he heard the smack of the wood and felt the vibration running up the bones of his arms. "Leave her alone!" he cried again, and the next words came out as hard punches of air. "She's—!" *Whack!* "—my—!" *Whack!* "—mother!"

Gordon, his cheekbones swollen and his nose bloody, staggered at the final blow. His toes remained on the platform, but his heels were over the edge. His eyes widened like those of a man who just realized his heart had stopped beating. He wavered, teetered, fell back, his arms pinwheeling for balance, the gun a glittering circle of light as it spun. Moxley managed to hook one arm around a girder. He almost certainly would have plunged to the ground, but at the last instant he wrapped his other arm around the girder and hugged it to him. Still holding the gun, he hung there, swinging gently seven stories above the earth. Mattie knelt down and gripped Moxley's arm. He heard the man's raspy breath, but Moxley seemed to take in the situation, eyeing first the girder, then Mattie, then the ground below.

He tried angling the gun at Mattie's nose. "Pull me up," Moxley said.

Mattie swallowed. "Drop the gun."

Moxley pulled back the hammer. The sound of it, loud even in the heavy, moist air, left a ringing in Mattie's ear. Mattie's hands trembled, but he squeezed the man's arm more tightly to remind Moxley of his circumstances.

"If you shoot me," Mattie said, "no one will help you, and you'll fall."

Moxley looked again at the girder and the platform. His arm muscles flexed—Mattie could feel them—as though the man were trying to haul himself up, but the arm wrapped around the girder was bandaged. To pull himself up, he would need his other hand—the one holding the gun. Moxley grunted, trying to swing his legs up.

A clatter of footsteps came from below. Voices called Mattie's name. "Over here!" Mattie shouted back.

Jake's head was the first to poke through the opening. He climbed up, with Peter following behind him. A moment later Byte and Robin came through. They helped Carla Marcetti to her feet while the two boys hurried over to give Mattie a hand.

"You doing okay?" Jake asked.

"Fine," said Mattie, "but I bet *his* arm's getting a charlie horse."

Gordon Moxley whimpered and looked down, so Mattie knew he'd made his point. The man was no longer pointing the gun at anyone in particular, yet he still would not release it.

Sirens wailed in the distance, and moments later two police cars with flashing lights pulled up to the building. A third car, a sedan with a single red light flashing on the roof over the driver's seat, pulled up behind them. Mattie recognized it as Decker's.

From the street, one of the uniformed officers trained his car's spotlight on the building. Decker and the other officers clambered up the rickety ladders toward the seventh floor, and Mattie could even hear Decker himself shout a mild obscenity when he banged his knee or hit an iffy section of plywood.

Gordon Moxley saw and heard it all. His fingers opened, and the gun fell from his hand and tumbled toward the earth. On the way down, it caught the light now and then and glittered, as though someone had tossed diamonds into the air one stone at a time. Mattie heard the thud when the gun buried itself in the dirt.

Gordon Moxley's voice was like the gravel far below. "You win," he said. "Pull me up."

epilogue

m attie wore his jeans today, the ones with the hole in the left knee. He also had on his favorite T-shirt, his most comfortable pair of sweat socks, and his oldest pair of sneakers—the ones with the black canvas tops that had grayed from years of sun exposure. He liked the way he could kick his feet together and watch little clouds of dust burst from the sneaker's fabric. These clothes made up an outfit—no, an *ensemble*—chosen especially for today. Last night he had set them out, draping them across a bedroom chair so he wouldn't have to search for them in the morning.

Mattie slammed his locker shut and headed down the hallway. In his hand was a lumpy package covered in baby-blue gift wrap. Dotting the gift wrap were pictures of brightly colored balloons. A string dangled from each balloon, and hanging onto the string was a tiny clown, who waved as though the balloon had just hoisted him off his feet and into the air.

Mattie scanned the lockers in the sophomore hallway until he found the person he was looking for. He strode up behind Heather Connelly just as she gave the dial on her locker a spin. She pulled up on the handle, but the locker refused to open.

"You have to go past the first number a couple of times before it'll work," he said.

Heather turned at the sound of his voice. She smiled at him, but she looked the same as always—hair hurriedly pulled back in a headband, face pale and without makeup, skin under the eyes dark and puffy.

"Hi, Mattie," she said.

He handed the package to her. "It's for Tyler."

Heather took the package slowly, touching it with just the tips of her fingers as though she were terrified it might break. "Mattie, that's so sweet," she said. "I don't know what to say. Should I open it now?"

Mattie nodded.

She tore off the paper, revealing a toy car with a blue body and huge red tires. Sitting behind the wheel of the car was a mommy with yellow plastic hair and painted face. In the passenger seat next to her was a male figure, smaller than the mommy and clearly intended to be the son. He was wearing a little plastic baseball cap.

"Let me show you what it does," Mattie said.

He took the toy and rolled it gently across the floor. It made music as the tires turned. The mommy's head swung back and forth, clicking as it did, and her hands moved the steering wheel.

"It's adorable!" Heather cried.

Mattie handed the toy back to her. "I was wondering," he said, "if maybe I could come over sometime. You know, just hang out. Maybe play with Tyler a little bit. I'll show him how to hit a curve ball."

Heather laughed. "He's nine months old," she said. "And can *you* hit a curve ball?"

Mattie folded his arms, feigning anger. "Well, no," he admitted, "but I want to tell you that wasn't a very nice question."

Heather turned one of the wheels with her hand. Music tinkled with each turn. "Sure," she said. "Anytime. You want to come by this afternoon?"

Mattie shook his head. "I can't," he told her. "I sort of have a date."

Heather nudged him. "Whoo hoo," she said.

Mattie laughed. "Nah—not that kind of a date. Tomorrow okay?"

"Sure."

He found his friends a few minutes later. Peter was standing at the pay phone in the school lobby, laughing goofily. *Goofily? Peter?* Even stranger, Robin was leaning into him, saying nothing at all. Jake stood nearby, his arm slung across Byte's shoulder as though it had always been there and didn't particularly care to ever leave.

Mattie frowned. "Stuff happened while I was away," he said.

"Okay," Peter said into the handset, "okay. Thanks, Lieutenant." He hung up the phone and turned to the others. "Decker's been questioning a guard at the prison. She's admitted feeding information to Moxley." He smiled. "Even better, Marco Weese matched the DNA of a hair inside the car we found at Seabreeze to Terrell Briggs. He pleaded guilty to second-degree murder about an hour ago."

"What about Gordon Moxley?" asked Byte.

"With Briggs's testimony, they're nailing him for everything," Peter said. "Gun charges, drug charges—" He looked at Mattie. "And a single count of attempted murder. Hey, Mattie. Didn't see you come up. Did you hear that?"

"Yeah, great news," Mattie said. "By the way, thanks, guys. Thanks for hanging in there."

Byte hugged him.

"Hey, we're going to catch a movie," said Robin. "You're coming too, right?"

Mattie shook his head. "Can't today," he said. "I have something planned."

He said good-bye to his friends and headed toward one of the glass doors at the front of the school. Punching the crash bar with the heel of his hand, he felt a blast of warmth against his face. It felt for a moment as though the air-conditioned building were sucking in a wave of heat from the outdoors, and the wave passed over Mattie as he stood there. He let the door slam shut, like a vacuum seal, and the feeling left him. He stood on the steps, shivered at the sudden change in temperature—or was it something else?—and headed down the concrete steps.

He walked toward a small residential park just down the street. As he approached, he could hear children shouting at each other in a sand-filled play area, laughing in high-pitched squeals. He saw a young man hurl a Frisbee and watched as a golden retriever leaped up to catch it in its mouth. He noted the row of cars parked in the few spaces along the street. One of them was a 1982 Chevy Malibu.

His mother sat at a picnic table.

When she saw him approach, she rose, but she didn't move toward him. She waited for him to come to her. For some reason, he found himself walking more slowly the closer he came. When he stood about three feet away, he stopped.

"Hi," she said.

"Hi."

This, Mattie thought, was the right sort of moment for talking with his mother. He was wearing his favorite clothes. The sun warmed their faces, a breeze blew their hair, and a bag full of greasy-sloppy burgers and french fries sat on a picnic table before them. No fancy restaurant. No stiff clothes. Even Carla had worn blue jeans. She wore no makeup, and her skin looked fresh and clean and pretty, Mattie thought.

And maybe a little pale. Mattie wondered if he was pale too.

"You want to sit?" she asked.

Mattie nodded. They somehow ended up sitting next to each other on the bench instead of across from each other. Neither spoke for a long time.

"Um…I heard," said Carla, "that you're really good at magic. You want to show me a magic trick?"

Mattie took a french fry from the bag and held it right up in front of Carla's face. He clapped his hands together, she blinked at the noise, and the bit of food was gone. Mattie was chewing.

"That's good," she said. "That's really good. I thought you were going to, I don't know, pull a quarter out of my ear or something. But that was better."

More silence. Carla looked out over the park. She seemed to be taking in the trees, the children, the bright sun in the distance. "So," she said. "You want to…ask me anything now?"

Mattie thought. He could ask a million complicated questions—questions that, if he wrote even one of them out, would be the length of an essay. He decided to take all of these, every one of the million, and stick them into one single question. Let Carla sort out the complications.

"Why?" he whispered.

His mother's arm moved slowly—so slowly he might not have noticed it. It landed, feather light, across his shoulder. When it had lain there a moment, as though it had tested its right to be there, the weight of it grew. Mattie stiffened uncomfortably at the gesture's intimacy, but soon he found himself relaxing, leaning into it.

"Okay," his mother whispered back. "Let's start there."